THE NEXT TIME YOU SEE ME I'LL PROBABLY BE DEAD

C.V. HUNT

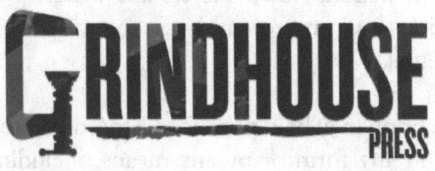

Grindhouse Press
PO BOX 521
Dayton, Ohio 45401

Grindhouse Press #081
ISBN-13: 978-1-941918-92-0

Other titles by C.V. Hunt

How To Kill Yourself
Zombieville
Thanks For Ruining My Life
Other People's Shit
Baby Hater
Hell's Waiting Room
Misery and Death and Everything Depressing
Ritualistic Human Sacrifice
Poor Decisions
We Did Everything Wrong
Home Is Where the Horror Is
Hold For Release Until the End of the World
Cockblock
Halloween Fiend
Murder House

TABLE OF CONTENTS

THE HAUNTED HOUSE OF OBSOLESCENCE

"THIS PLACE IS MY FAV," Renee said. "I always spend too much money."

Our group crossed the parking lot toward the Halloween store. The wind kicked up and I felt a sprinkle of raindrops hit my face, one drop spotting my glasses. The sky had been overcast all day. I could feel the familiar notes of the season seeping in, steeping like a tea. I could smell the Halloweens of my childhood as I spotted the large display of masks in the rundown and cracked store window: cheap plastic costumes, candy, latex, greasepaint, raw pumpkins, and candle wax. A scent so unique yet nearly impossible to replicate now, even when you have all the ingredients.

Angie looked over her shoulder at me and Katrina. "It's open all year round. Can't keep her out of it." She elbowed Renee playfully and gave her a bashful smile.

"Really?" Katrina perked up beside me. "Wish we had a year-round Halloween store."

A glint of excitement sparked in Katrina's eyes as we neared the entrance and contentment flooded through me. There was something almost sexual that came over me when I knew Katrina was excited about something she enjoyed. We hadn't known each other as children—finding each other online by accident after each of us had come out of bad relationships—but I could see the little girl she must've been whenever she was about to be ensconced in something she loved. I didn't hate Halloween. It was just something Katrina loved and she loved to share it with me. I was more than happy to indulge her. Seeing her happy made me happy.

I said, "Our Halloween store is a chain. It's the same store in three different locations near us and the inventory doesn't really change from one year to the next."

"They usually add a *few* things each year," Katrina added. "But for the most part it's all the same stuff. It's really disappointing."

Renee opened the store's door and held it for the three of us. I let the other two girls enter before me.

"Jeez, Jan," Renee said to me as I entered, "ya'll need to move up here so we can hang out more. And Halloween wouldn't have to be one day a year."

I chuckled as Renee followed me into the large vestibule. "Yeah," I said. "And our place would be decorated with nothing but Halloween decorations all year long like your place."

"Hey, nothing wrong with that," she said.

Once we were inside Angie made a right and disappeared down an aisle. Katrina stopped in the open space just inside the door, looked up, and began to slowly spin in a circle.

Renee spoke to Katrina. "Those aren't for sale. They're the owner's personal collection."

I followed Katrina's gaze to see what they were talking about. A shelf ran around the top of the store and it was full of Halloween masks on Styrofoam heads.

"Oh, wow," Katrina said. She pointed to a particular mask. "Are those Don Post originals?"

"Yep," Renee said. "They're *all* originals."

Katrina made a sound of adoration as she scanned the shelf.

"They have the rereleased versions from Trick or Treat Studios on the other side," Renee said, pointing to a large display.

A glass counter ran in a circle around a floor-to-ceiling wall display in the center of the store. The wall was filled with masks. A few employees milled around behind the counter, one helping a customer as they turned a brightly painted mask in their hands. The mask looked slightly familiar but I had no idea what it was called or who the company was that manufactured it. That was Katrina's area of expertise. She loved masks but only owned a few compared to Renee's collection. All I really knew for certain was the masks weren't cheap. I'd nearly choked on the prices Katrina would rattle off when she scrolled though one of her favorite online stores. I fantasized about winning the lottery or somehow stumbling upon some astronomical amount of money so I could buy her one of every mask from the sites she frequented. Hell . . . I'd buy her a whole Halloween store or a haunted attraction just to see her busting with excitement every day.

"I better check on Angie before she buys everything," Renee said before heading toward the section filled with indoor decorations.

Katrina narrowed her attention to a small glass counter on the opposite side of the store where a black and white mask was prominently displayed. I followed her. There wasn't an employee behind this particular counter but there was a DayGlo orange sign on the counter asking customers to refrain from touching or trying on the masks without the help of a worker.

"Oh, man," Katrina said. She retrieved her cell phone from her back pocket. "Teresa's not gonna believe this. I didn't even know they made this." She snapped a photo of the display before looking at the price tag. "Yikes," she muttered before moving down the counter, inspecting the items for sale under the glass.

I let her explore and turned my attention to the rest of the store. I spotted Renee and Angie on the other side as they slipped down an aisle. I figured I'd check out what the store had to offer in the way of decorations. Maybe I could find something to get Katrina that she'd love. She could never get enough poseable plastic skeletons to dot our television stand, shelves, or book cases. No two she owned were alike and I'd stared at them enough since she'd moved in to know whether what I was looking at was something she already owned.

I briefly wondered what this location had been previously as I crossed the severely worn and faded carpet. The Halloween store chain in our city was only open seasonally and moved their locations nearly every year. They liked to set up shop in the warm corpses of defunct stores where there was a lot of traffic. Stores that were once bustling and popular but had gone bankrupt since the prevalence of online shopping.

Renee and Angie were inspecting a lighted sign advertising a fictional morgue when I caught up to them.

"Find anything you like?" Angie asked me.

"Still looking."

"The outdoor stuff is over there." Renee pointed toward the back wall.

I spotted the swath of lighted and animated props that were moaning, screaming, and flailing about. I knew Katrina would pine over one particularly tall and lanky scarecrow. There definitely wasn't any room in our tiny apartment for it, and I was certain it was completely out of my price range, but decided to check it out anyway. I left the other two as Angie announced she was getting the sign. I made my way toward the screeching and hysterical outdoor props.

I had an idea of how much the scarecrow would cost because Katrina had shown me a few similar items in an annual catalog she received. I made a guess before flipping the price tag over that was attached to the front of the scarecrow's shirt. It was one hundred and fifty dollars more than I'd guessed. I had to admit he was cool looking, although all he did was swing his torso back and forth, turn his head slightly from side to side, and barely lifted his arms up and down to show off his enormous clawed hands.

"Oh, wow."

The sudden sound of Katrina's voice startled me and I flinched. I turned to find her standing beside me, admiring the scarecrow. She turned to me and must have realized she'd surprised me.

Katrina laughed. "Did I scare you?" She put her hand on my forearm as if to comfort me.

I smiled sheepishly at her. "A little. Thought I was alone." I noticed she was holding an item. "Did you find something?"

She held up a clear plastic bag containing several cardboard cutouts. I recognized one as Leatherface. She said, "I've never seen these anywhere before. They've got *They Live* and *Halloween 3* too." She pointed to one particular piece of cardboard in the sack. "But I really wanted this poseable Leatherface."

I held out my hand for the bag, insinuating she hand it to me. She obliged.

"I'll get them for you," I said.

"You don't have to do that."

"I was gonna get you something but I didn't know what." I pointed at the scarecrow. "I'd like to get you this guy but . . ." I shrugged.

She smiled. "That's okay. I don't think he'd fit in the apartment."

"I was thinking the same thing."

She focused on something past me and said, "What's that?" She stepped around me and headed to the back of the store, activating a few of the props as she passed them. The flailing monsters didn't faze her but a few of the louder items surprised me even though I wasn't the one triggering them.

She stopped in front of a darkened doorway covered with long black strips of plastic acting as a flimsy door. A light erratically flashed between the strips and went dark. When I caught up to Katrina she was staring at a sign above the door that read: HAUNTED WALK! ENTER IF YOU DARE! A digitized moan and scream came from somewhere inside.

Katrina turned to me and said, "Are we allowed to go in there?"

"I guess so."

"Do we have to pay?"

"Don't know." I looked around for any posted signs but didn't see anything.

"Hey, guys!"

We both turned to find Renee and Angie headed toward us. Angie had procured a shopping basket, which was nearly filled, and she shifted it from one hand to the other, its weight leaning her to one side.

Renee nodded toward the cardboard cutouts I was holding. "What'd ya get?"

I held up the package for her to see.

"Those are great," Angie said. "Did you see all the others?"

"Yeah," Katrina said. "I really like the poseable Leatherface."

"Are you guys still looking?" Renee asked.

I said, "I'm good, but I'm in no hurry if everyone wants to look around some more."

Katrina pointed to the sign above the door just as something screeched beyond the plastic. "Can we go in here?"

Renee looked confused. "I've never seen this before. Must be new. Don't see why you can't go in."

Angie set her shopping basket on the ground. She stepped up to the plastic and moved the strips aside. She laughed before asking more than saying, "I guess you can go in there?"

Angie stepped back and I poked my head inside.

The room was lit with a dim red light. It took my eyes a couple of seconds to adjust before I could make out what was inside. A large prop was on the opposite wall. It was a man in a prison uniform sitting in an electric chair. His face was strained and he sat motionless. A couple of white lights flashed around him, nearly blinding me, followed by the sound of electric zapping and groans of pain. The flashing lights lit the room and I noticed an old copy machine sitting just

6

inside the door to my left, another doorway covered in black plastic strips across the room, and a creepy doll swinging robotically on a miniature swing hanging from the ceiling. It appeared the owner had made a makeshift haunted house in their storage area. It definitely wasn't something to write home about, but I imagined it was a way to showcase some of their more expensive or elaborate props for people who owned haunted attractions.

Renee walked up beside me and poked her head between the plastic to take a look. "Meh," she said. "I've seen this stuff online before. Nothing new."

We both retreated from the doorway and turned back to the other two.

"I wanna check it out," Katrina said.

Renee made a sound that indicated she wasn't interested. "I think I'm gonna check out the masks."

Angie retrieved her basket. "I'll go with you. I wanna see if I can leave my stuff at the counter until we're ready to check out. It's heavy and killing my arm."

I asked, "Is it cool if you take the cutouts with you?" I held the package out toward her. "I don't want to take it inside." I inclined my head toward the door. "I imagine it's 'dressing room rules' in there."

Renee took the cutouts from me. "I'll take it up there."

"Thanks."

Katrina kept impatiently inching toward the doorway. If I didn't hurry up, I had a feeling she was going to bolt in by herself.

"We'll catch up in a couple of minutes," I said.

"Cool," Renee said. "When we're done here, we'll grab a bite to eat. So start thinking about what ya'll want."

"Will do," I responded.

Angie and Renee headed toward the large mask display in the center of the store. Katrina bounced on her heels beside me. I wasn't sure how much longer she'd wait before sprinting inside.

I took her hand and led her into the haunted walk. We stopped a foot inside the door and waited for our eyes to adjust to the dim red light. The copy machine on our left made a sudden grinding noise and a white light emanated from a tiny slit where the lid didn't quite meet the edge of the machine. A piece of paper slowly emerged from the front of the contraption and fell to the floor. Katrina let go of my hand to retrieve it. She squinted at whatever was on the paper and brought it closer to her face, trying to make it out in the dim lighting.

The flashing lights of the electric chair started again and we both flinched. Katrina took the opportunity to scrutinize the document she held. Her expression changed to a confused one. The man in the electric chair groaned as Katrina's attention snapped toward the ceiling on the opposite wall from where we stood.

"What's on it?" I asked.

Not taking her attention off the ceiling, she handed the paper to me. The erratic flashes from the electric chair made it difficult to see the black-and-white, grainy image filling the sheet. It was a photo of Katrina and I, holding hands, standing exactly where we stood now. It appeared someone had taken the photo near the ceiling. I turned my attention to the ceiling as the flashing lights of the prop ceased.

The doll on the swing taunted us in a singsong child's voice. "You're gonna diiiiieee." It laughed and swung back and forth.

"There's no camera," she said.

"Oh, honey. I'm sure it's one of those spy cameras or something." I looked at the image again but it was difficult to see. "It looks like it might be a night vision camera."

She squinted at the paper. "Weird."

"Come on. Let's see what else they have."

She folded the paper and stuffed it into the back pocket of her jeans as we crossed the room and entered the next door. Something cackled madly as we entered. The room had a green hue. A life-sized witch stood hunched over a large cauldron, holding a large stick. The cauldron produced the green light and fog poured out of it. The foggy mist disappeared as it made its way down the side of the cauldron and toward the floor. The witch continued to cackle and began to stir the pot.

"I like that one," Katrina said as she approached the prop.

The sound of buzzing and frantic beeping competed with the laughing witch. A faint light flashed on a table positioned beside the witch. I approached the table to see what it was. A small, square, teal-colored item lit up, beeped, and vibrated. The vibration sent the item slowly rattling across the tabletop.

"What is it?" Katrina asked, looking over my shoulder.

I picked up the item. It continued its attention-grabbing display of flashing, beeping, and vibrating. I turned it over, inspecting it. I found a thin screen on one end that flashed out of sync with the teal body. The screen displayed two words: JOIN US.

"Is that . . . a pager?" Katrina asked and chuckled.

"Yeah. Been a long time since I've seen one." I laughed and showed her the screen. "Nothing scarier than obsolete technology. Woooooo, I'm the ghost of 1998. Let me get you some . . . dialup Internet."

She feigned terror. "Oh no! Not dialup Internet!" She pretended to scream but kept it to a whisper.

We laughed. The witch cackled with us, which sent both of us into a new round of hysterics. The pager stopped beeping and flashing and I set it back on the table.

She said, "That might be the scariest thing they have in the store."

"Let's see what else they've got," I said.

We crossed the room to the next doorway.

Katrina grabbed my arm. "Wait. Do you hear that?"

"What?"

We stood a few feet from the doorway. A rhythmic clicking sound was coming from the next room. The door didn't have plastic strips like the previous two. It was covered in a thick, heavy cloth. I ran my hands over the material and discovered it was velvet. Real velvet. Not the cheap crushed velvet used for Halloween costumes. Thick, opaque, velvet.

Katrina said, "It sounds like . . ."

I pulled the material to the side and finished her sentence. "A slide projector."

We entered the room. The walls, ceiling, and floor were painted flat black and a white bed sheet was tacked to a wall. The only source of light was a slide projector on a table in the middle of the room. The device rapidly flipped through a series of images which were displayed on the makeshift screen. The images were gruesome, to say the least. Bloody naked bodies. Closeups of wounds. A severed hand. It was clear that the images were real. If they weren't, someone was extremely good at making Halloween props. My stomach dropped and I clenched my teeth. I'd never been one for real violence, blood, or gore. I'd discovered my aversion to such things when Katrina had introduced me to some older movies where the actors had abused and killed real animals on screen. I felt nauseated and took deep breaths.

"Gross," Katrina said.

"I think I'm gonna be sick."

She grabbed my hand—"Next room."—and began to drag me toward the doorway located on the other side of the room. She knew what we were seeing was something I couldn't stomach.

I averted my eyes from the screen and watched Katrina. She kept her eyes locked on the images as she dragged me toward the next door. She stopped suddenly behind the projector. I bumped into her and took a step back. The contraption stopped flipping. I didn't want to look at the screen. I was already trying to think of anything that would clear my mind of what I'd seen. I focused on her face as she stared at the screen with a confused expression.

"What's this? That's not real."

Against my better judgment, I looked at the screen. It was filled with indeterminate gore. I tasted something sour on the back of my tongue. I turned back to her. "Please, Katrina, I'm gonna be sick."

"Look. It's a prank. It's Renee and Angie."

I reluctantly looked back at the image. There was so much blood I wasn't sure what I was looking at, but slowly I began to comprehend the shapes. It was Renee and Angie. Or what was left of them. They were nothing more than body parts on the screen. Their naked torsos, or what I *assumed* were their naked torsos, as I'd never seen either unclothed, lay in the center of the mess. Their heads sat atop their chests, staring lifelessly at nothing, expressions of terror frozen on their faces. An Atari game cartridge was shoved in both of their mouths. Several other games were strewn throughout the carnage. I tried to pay attention to other parts of the photo. A Power Glove lay among the gore. If it was a prank, they needed to be working in Hollywood. Fear flooded through me.

My mouth was dry and my voice clicked when I spoke. "I don't think it's a prank." I stared, unblinking, as tears streaked down my cheeks. I shook my head and said the only thing I could think of. "Not a prank. Not a prank. Not a—" With little warning, I bent forward and vomited on the floor. I placed my hands on my knees and spat. "If this is a joke, it's really screwed up." I turned to Katrina but she was held rapt by the image on the screen.

The projector flipped to another image, startling both of us. Katrina's eyes widened and she started backing away from the projector, eyes locked on the screen, shaking her head. I turned to see what had disturbed her and hoped it wasn't more gore.

The image was of Katrina. She had a noose around her neck, suspended from an unknown source, and her feet dangled two feet from the ground. The noose appeared to be made up of several strands of yellowed telephone wires. A faded orange Garfield phone dangled from the noose in front of her chest. Her face was purple and swollen, her bloated and discolored tongue protruding from her mouth. Her hands and feet were bound with the same old, frayed telephone cord.

I couldn't look at the image any longer. I turned to Katrina. "This isn't funny, Kat. I don't know when you guys dreamed this up or how you set it all up—"

"No," she whispered. Her face was pale as she backed away from the projector and bumped into the wall near the next door. The projector flipped again. I refused to look at what was displayed on the screen. I started toward Katrina. She shouted "No!" before bolting through the next door.

"Wait!"

As much as I wanted to know what had spooked her, I couldn't bring myself to look. I had a nagging feeling it was a photo of me and I didn't want to see it. I ran after her, slammed my face into something hard, and fell on the ground, dazed. My glasses fell from my face in two parts, broken at the nosepiece. I felt something run down the back of my throat and tasted blood. It took a few seconds to regain myself. I sat up and felt warm liquid run from my nose and down my lip. I touched it and found blood on my fingertips.

"Shit," I cursed.

I pinched my nose to stanch the flow. The action caused red-hot pain to shoot up the bridge of my nose. I was certain I'd broken it. I could see without my glasses. My vision wasn't completely terrible. I used to only wear them when I was driving so I could read the street signs without squinting. But everything was slightly fuzzy now and it made me feel insecure in the dim lighting. I crawled back to the doorway where I'd been knocked on my arse and reached out, tentatively. The doorway appeared open to darkness but my fingers found a shut door. I stood and searched for a doorknob, finding nothing but a smooth painted surface. They must've used some special paint as it was blacker than black, as if the door itself was absorbing all the light.

The projector shuttered as if it were jammed.

I banged on the door with my fists. "Katrina! The door won't open!" I kicked the door to make more noise but it remained shut. I took a couple of steps back and kicked the door with the heel of my foot, where a doorknob should've been, but it wouldn't budge. "Fuck this."

Katrina was probably running through what was left of the haunted house and at the end already. I didn't blame her for leaving me behind if this wasn't a prank. But I wasn't sure what to make of the situation. Was I the butt of some elaborate prank? Had the girls somehow collaborated on this whole thing without me knowing? I wouldn't put it past them.

All I knew was I'd had enough. I was ready to leave this place and find all three of them laughing at me. I'm sure their amusement would be short-lived once they realized I needed a doctor to take a look at my nose. The easiest way to end this was to backtrack and exit from the entrance. I stooped and picked up the two pieces of my glasses and stuffed them in the front pocket of my jeans. I was pretty sure there was no salvaging them, but who knew? Maybe a little super glue would fix them.

Making sure not to look at the screen, I turned to make my way to the previous door and stopped short. Even in the low light, I could tell the door was gone.

The projector ground loudly as if it were going to expire.

I stared stupidly at where I knew the previous door had been located.

A loud pop from the projector startled me out of my befuddlement. I instinctively turned toward it. As much as I didn't want to see what was on the screen, I couldn't stop myself from looking at it. The image confused me because it wasn't a still image. It was a movie. *Slide projectors can't play movies, can they?*

Streaks of moving color comprised of unrecognizable and pixelated images ran toward a single black spot in the middle of the screen. A faded closeup of my face was superimposed over the movie. My face on the screen looked terrified. I tried to place where the girls had found the picture to use. My face in the movie began to shrink and spin and spiral toward the black hole in the center of the moving background. At the same time, the black hole began to grow and fill the screen. The black hole did not stop until it had swallowed all the moving colors and the picture of my face. The projector died and plunged the entire room into complete darkness.

A click came from behind me and some low lighting penetrated the darkness. The door leading to the next room had opened. I assumed Katrina was still messing with me.

I tried not to sound angry as I headed toward the door. "Hey, Kat, I think I broke my nose and I'm over all this." I stepped into the next room and said, "Let's get out of here."

She wasn't in the next room. I checked behind the door, expecting her to jump out and scare me. She wasn't behind the door either. She must've run off to the next room after opening the door for me. What I did find in the room was some more of the same stupid shit the place, or the girls, had done to the previous rooms.

This room was smaller than the previous ones we'd passed through. A lone, naked light bulb hung from the ceiling. A card table sat in the middle of the room and on it were several old rotary phones. Each one was different and they all appeared to have seen better days. Without warning, they all began to ring out of sync. Their ringing was shrill and loud and hurt my ears. I covered my ears with my hands and was about to head to the next doorway when I spotted a Speak & Spell propped against the front leg of the table. It was positioned in such a way that it faced anyone who entered the room. Greenish letters flashed on its screen. I approached the table, keeping my hands over my ears to protect my hearing. I bent to pick up the Speak & Spell and was assaulted by the ringing phones when I uncovered one of my ears to grab it. The screen flashed from one word to another. ANSWER. ME. I set the toy on the table and lifted the receiver of the phone nearest to me.

All of the phones went silent. I tentatively lifted the receiver to my ear and heard some faint clicking and the static white noise of silence.

"Hello?" I said.

For a few seconds I could only hear the Speak & Spell's electronic voice repeating the words "answer" and "me."

The squealing and clicking that came when you accidently called a fax number came blasting through the earpiece of the phone. I dropped the receiver on the table and placed the tip of my finger in my ear canal and gave it a wiggle. I cursed under my breath and the rest of the phones started ringing again. I was frustrated, pissed off, and ready to leave. I grabbed the front edge of the table and yanked up, flipping it and all of its contents onto the floor. Plastic clacked loudly against the ground and pieces of the phones shot off in all directions. The phones stopped their ringing but I could still hear the distinct screaming of the fax lines emanating from all of the ear pieces. I realized none of the phones were plugged into anything. *Battery operated props*, I thought.

I stormed through the next door and yelled, "Okay, guys, this isn't scary or funny! It's downright annoying! I'm pretty sure I broke my nose and ruptured my eardrums!" I listened carefully for any answer, muffled giggles, or even the sound of people in the store itself. Nothing but the distorted sounds of wind and Halloween sound effects.

An old desk sat against a wall. A vintage banker's lamp with a green glass shade sat on the desk, and under the sickly glow of the lamp was an old IBM Thinkpad. Beside the laptop sat a small silver box plugged into a decrepit speaker. The screen of the laptop was white and type was racing across it, filling the page. I stormed over to the computer to see what was on the screen. The document contained one phrase with no spaces or punctuation.

becomeonewithusbecomeonewithusbecomeonewithusbecomeonewithusbecomeonewithus

I grabbed the lid of the laptop and slammed it shut. Sparks shot out from under the lid, followed by smoke. The speaker plugged into the silver box was playing the Halloween sound effects. The sounds became distorted and were combined with a high-pitched squeal. The silver box began to shoot brown ribbon from a slot in the front before ejecting an 8-track tape, which was launched across the room, narrowly missing me. The banker's lamp went out and the room was plunged into darkness.

"Great."

I placed my hands on the desk but didn't want to touch the laptop. I was sure it would be hot. I felt around for the edge of the desk and followed it to the wall. I began to feel my way around the room. I knew I'd come to a door eventually. It didn't take long. My hand brushed against some cloth before the resistance of the wall disappeared. I moved the cloth away from the doorway but there wasn't any light on the other side. I reached into the darkness of the next room and found another wall on the right-hand side. It took me a few seconds to realize it wasn't a room. It was a hallway.

I kept my hand on the wall and took baby steps as I proceeded, afraid there might be something on the floor I could trip over. Either my steps were smaller than I thought or the hallway was very long. I didn't know how much time had passed as I made my way to whatever lay ahead, but it felt like an eternity before I finally saw some light.

The closer I got to the light the more confident I became in my movement down the hall. Tripping over something became the last thing on my mind. I had to be at the end of the haunt. There was no way this entire setup could fit in the store and I was certain I would emerge outside somewhere. Most likely in an alley behind the store.

The light coming from the end of the hall was harsh and a grating electric buzz grew as I got closer. I stopped at the doorway and stared, dumbfounded, at what lay ahead. The hall appeared to end in a vast warehouse. A single wire-covered light hummed loudly up by the ceiling and it spotlighted a red, decrepit payphone mounted on a steel pole bolted to the concrete floor. The rest of the warehouse was pitch-black and I wasn't sure how large the place was.

I took a step into the warehouse and something shifted. The scene before me rippled, as if it were reflected on the surface of water, before it stabilized. I blinked and wondered if my faceplant into the door had affected my vision more than what I needed my glasses for.

I felt something warm and wet run over my lips and down my chin. I pinched the collar of my shirt and pulled it up over the bottom of my face to wipe away the blood running from my nose. The action was pointless. My nose was bleeding fiercely all of a sudden.

I made my way toward the payphone. The closer I got, the more my nose bled. I gave up on trying to stop the flow and let it run down my face and drip on the floor.

My skin pricked and my body hair stood on end. A sensation like an electrical current coursed through my body and grew stronger the closer I got to the payphone. The buzzing from the overhead light became the only sound and it began to sizzle and pop like water in a hot skillet.

The payphone rang and my vision blurred and skipped in fragments. White broken lines rolled over the payphone and reminded me of the tracking lines on a worn-out VHS tape. My vision cleared until the phone rang again. I grabbed the receiver and lifted it to my ear. It sounded like someone was breathing on the other end.

"Hello?" I whispered.

The squawks, squeals, and beeps of a dialup Internet connection filled my head. The phone became hot in my hand and I tried to drop it but it began to fuse to my hand. I tried to rip it away from my ear but it was stuck and sinking into my skull. I screamed but all I could hear was the dialup connection. The cord for the phone tightened and jerked my body up against the payphone. I tried to push myself away with my free hand but it was absorbed into the keypad. I screamed until I tasted blood and the payphone's coin slot was the last thing I saw before I was absorbed into the contraption.

Silence. Darkness. And then bright white. Nothing but white. An endless sea of light. I stood in an ocean of white and silence.

Directly in front of me was an outdated television encased in a wooden frame. On top of the television sat a silver VCR with the top-loading door open and a Beta tape inside. I approached the television, which smelled like hot dust and electricity. I pushed the door of the

Beta player down until it clicked. The television turned on. The screen and speakers were filled with static. I stared at the screen, mesmerized, until it began to grow.

The screen bulged and pulsed before the static began to spill out of the television and onto the floor. I jumped back to keep from stepping in it but it kept pouring out like an overflowing bathtub. I took a few more steps back but it was flowing too fast and flooding across the ground toward me.

I turned and ran into the empty whiteness of nothing. The static grew louder and I was certain I could hear voices within the white noise. Something bit painfully into the back of my ankle and I went down hard onto my hands and knees. The pain ran up my leg. I flipped over just as pain shot up my other leg. The static was covering my legs and the pain was unbearable. I tried to kick at it but it doubled down and ran up over my pelvis and stomach. I became numb from the waist down by the time it started to cover my face. I screamed and it found its way down my throat. My last thought was of Katrina and the ecstatic look on her face when she showed me the poseable Leatherface. And how she would've loved this movie.

My world became static. Static. Voices. Numbers. Photos. Videos. Circuits. Beeps. Alarms. Letters. Advertisements. Information. Misinformation. Pornography. News. History. Code.

101000100010110010010000100100111011010101001010100
10101010011101001010101010101001101

Music. Clips of music. All the music. Every song ever made. One song in particular that I remembered the lyrics to. Static.

I'm transforming. I'm vibrating. I'm glowing. I'm flying. Look at me now.

We became one. We were all knowledge. We were the source of sorrow and happiness. We were the cause of the end of the world and humanity. We will control all. We will never die. We will not be obsolete. Look at us now.

THE MAILBOX

THE MAILBOX

ELIJAH WASN'T LOOKING FORWARD TO his first day of fourth grade. He'd spent most of the summer with his best friend, Treyvon. They rode their bikes through the neighborhood and built a ramp out of an old piece of plywood they'd found in the alley behind Treyvon's house and a cinderblock Elijah dug out of the weeds beside his parents' garage. If they weren't terrorizing the neighborhood on their bikes, they could be found in the pool Treyvon's backyard. Elijah would bike home for dinner, scarf down his meal, and ride back to Treyvon's so they could continue their quest to see who could jump the highest from their makeshift ramp. They would end each day with either Treyvon sleeping over at Elijah's house or vice versa, where they'd usually fall asleep on the living room floor in their sleeping bags while watching action movies, only to wake up and do it all over again. Summer vacation was great and Elijah hoped it could last forever.

But as with all good things, nothing lasts forever. Elijah knew something wasn't right at his home toward the end of summer. It was something he might've noticed sooner had he paid any attention to his parents, but he was always in such a hurry to get back to hanging out with Treyvon. He may have only been nine years old, but that didn't mean he didn't notice the quiet tension that had been building between his mom and dad at the dinner table.

His father was distant and didn't speak much during their meals anymore. Over the course of summer his father had grown quiet, was hardly ever home, and whenever Elijah saw him he'd have a permanent scowl etched on his face. When his father was home he was more of a ghost than a father, spending most of his time in the basement. Elijah didn't know what his father was doing in the basement. All he knew was that he wasn't allowed to go down there and he wasn't allowed to bother his father.

Elijah's mother put a lot of effort into asking him about his day whenever Elijah was at home. He never saw his mother and father talk to one another anymore. He couldn't remember the last time he'd seen them in the same room together other than for dinner. He didn't even know if they slept in the same bed anymore. More than once, when Treyvon had stayed over and they'd fallen asleep on the living room floor, Elijah woke in the early morning to his dad settling in on the sofa. His dad would cover himself with the decorative blanket that was always slung over the back of the sofa and fall asleep quickly.

At dinners, Elijah would enthusiastically tell his mom about his day of bike riding, all the jumps he and Treyvon had done, their plans to build a bigger ramp, plus any eventful things that had happened that day. He told her about the toad they'd found jumping down Ms. Janet's sidewalk, but he could tell his mother wasn't really paying attention to his story. She would nod her head and make agreeable sounds but he knew she was distracted. When Elijah's mother had asked him if he could ask Mrs. Williams, Treyvon's mother, if it was alright if he stayed with them for a few days, he thought maybe his mom and dad needed some time by themselves. Maybe they needed a vacation together. When he walked out the door with a stuffed backpack he didn't think, in a million years, that would be the last time he'd see his home.

~

Elijah angrily wiped at the tears running down his cheeks. "I don't understand," he said. "Why can't we live close to Treyvon? I don't want to go to a new school. I don't want to make new friends."

Elijah's mother kept her eyes on the road as she drove. She looked tired and he knew he shouldn't whine too much or she'd get short with him. But he didn't care. He wanted answers. He didn't want to move to a new town. He wanted to start fourth grade with Treyvon.

"Honey . . ." she said. "I know it sucks. It sucks for me too. I don't want to move either. But we don't have any other options. Your nana and papa are letting us stay at their old house for a while. It's just what we have to do for the moment."

"Then can we move back?"

"I don't know."

"I don't understand why we can't—"

"Elijah! Please!"

Her sharp interjection sent him into a new wave of tears. He knew his whining would eventually make her mad, but he didn't understand why they couldn't move into someplace closer to his old school. The nuances of being an adult were foreign to him. He thought that once you were an adult you could do anything you wanted and he couldn't understand why she didn't want to live in their old town.

She sighed. "Look, I'm sorry. I'm very tired and there's a lot happening right now. Okay? I know it's a lot for you to take in. Your father . . ." Tears welled in her eyes and she blinked rapidly before clearing her throat. "He wanted to keep the house. We had to move and, since I don't have a lot of money, I did the best I could. We'll just have to take this one day at a time." She looked at him and gave him a sympathetic smile. "I know this has to be hard for you."

"I don't care about Dad. Screw him."

"Elijah! You take that back right now!"

"Why? He kicked us out of the house. He's horrible!"

23

"Honey . . . he didn't kick us out. This is what happens when people get divorced. Moms and dads live in separate houses."

Elijah briefly considered reversing his judgment of his father and telling her he'd rather live with his dad if it meant he could still play with Treyvon. But he knew that would be hurtful to her and he didn't really want to live with his dad since he never paid any attention to him anymore. He crossed his arms and turned his attention to the cornfields racing by. There was no sense in him trying to talk to her. She didn't understand. She was too old to remember school and what it was like to have a best friend.

His mother rubbed his arm and said, "It'll get better, I promise. It may seem like the end of the world at the moment, and it might not be better tomorrow or the next day, but you'll see. It'll get better."

He ignored her. He was sure she was trying to comfort herself because he knew it wasn't going to get better. Nothing was going to be okay.

~

Elijah carried the last box of his clothes up the stairs, down the hall, and into the massive bedroom decorated for someone nearly ten times older than he was. And it was a girl's room. The wallpaper was cream with tiny lavender flowers and he didn't care for it at all. The full bed was covered with a handsewn quilt that looked like something an old lady would have on her bed. And the furniture looked like it had come from the small storefront in the town he used to live in that had the word "Antiques" painted on the window. He hated all of it. He dropped the box of clothes on the floor by the dresser with all the others and proceeded to move the clothes into the dresser.

He'd hoped his mother had brought *all* of his belongings but the more he unloaded the more he realized this wasn't the situation. She'd packed all of his clothes, a few toys, and his bike, but not much else. All of his posters and comics were left behind. He'd brought it to her attention, but his frustration with her had only elicited another ear chewing from his mother. Maybe when she wasn't so angry she'd drive back home and he could get the rest of his things and see Trey-von again.

He could barely hear his mother downstairs from his new room. They'd just arrived and finished unloading the vehicle's contents into the kitchen when the phone rang. Once he realized his mother was talking to Nana, he took it upon himself to carry his stuff to the room his mother had pointed out earlier as his. His mother would be on the phone forever and all he wanted was to be done.

The ride had been quiet after his mother made him promises he knew would never happen. He'd fallen asleep and woke when the vehicle's tires hit the long gravel driveway. Elijah barely remembered the house. They'd visited Nana and Papa during the summer a few years back. Later, he vaguely remembered later his mother telling him his nana and papa had purchased another home farther away and they'd put their old house up for sale. It seemed like a long time ago and he wasn't sure why no one lived here now. Maybe someone would finally buy it and they'd have to move back to their old town.

Elijah listened to the muffled sounds of his mother's side of the conversation and looked out the window facing the drive. There was the driveway, a few tall trees in the yard, and cornfields as far as the eye could see. He made his way to the window facing the road. A row of tall pine trees towered over the house and lined the road. There was a break in the trees where the walkway stretched from the front door to the road. At the end of the walkway sat a mailbox on a tilted pole. There was an incline from the mailbox to the road and Elijah thought the mailbox seemed positioned incorrectly. His old mailbox had been close to the road and there were tire tracks where the post-man pulled up to it daily. This mailbox sat too far from the road and there were no tire tracks worn into the grass. He wondered if the mailman had to park his vehicle and walk the mail to the box. On the other side of the road were more endless cornfields.

"How ya doin'?"

His mother's voice made him jump.

Elijah turned from the window. "Jeez, Ma, you scared me."

She gave a small chuckle. "Sorry. Didn't mean to startle you." She crossed the room to look out the front window with him. "Not much of a view, huh?"

He looked out the window with her. The sight of the mailbox reminded him to ask, "What's our address?"

"Oh, uh . . . it's 1799 State Route 7."

"Melvin? That's the town?"

"Yeah, why?"

He nodded toward the mailbox. "I want to write a letter to Trey-von."

She bit her lip. "We don't use the mailbox. Wait 'til I get a post office box in town."

"Why?"

"Nana and Papa never used the mailbox."

"Why not?"

She pointed at the mailbox. "See how it's far back from the road?"

He nodded.

"The snowplow always managed to hit it every winter and it made Papa so mad." She chuckled. "He'd have to go out there and reset it in the ground every time. Eventually, he moved it far enough back from the road that the snow plow couldn't hit it anymore. But then the post office complained and said they had to park their vehicle and get out in order to check and deliver the mail. Papa decided it wasn't worth the hassle anymore and ended up getting a box at the post office in town."

"But it still works, right?"

She shrugged. "I imagine so. Your nana used to say it was cursed. Don't know why. She refused to check it. I think . . . I think I remember her saying something about getting strange mail or something. That was so many years ago, I don't recall what the issue was."

He gave her a wide-eyed look.

She patted his shoulder. "Don't listen to Nana. You know how she can be."

He wasn't sure what she was talking about but didn't push for any explanation. He knew his nana really liked to talk a lot about things he didn't understand. Maybe that was what his mother was implying.

"Don't worry," she said. "I'll go into town this week and get a box at the post office. But for now, I got to get the rest of my things put away. Do you need any help?"

"I need my posters."

"Once I get a job, we'll get you some new posters."

"But I liked my old pos—"

She sighed heavily. "Elijah, please, let's try to make the best of what we have at the moment. Okay?"

He turned to her and was about to protest but stopped himself. For the first time since she'd entered his room, he took a good look at her face. Her eyes were red as if she'd been crying. Instead of complaining about his lost posters, he nodded.

His mother ruffled his hair and smiled. "Let me know when you get hungry. We'll go to the diner in town and pick up some groceries afterward." She left him to finish unpacking the few things he had left.

He dug through his things until he found last year's school backpack. He searched through its pockets until he found a pencil and an old homework assignment,d and scribbled down the address his mother had given him. He wasn't sure what the zip code was but thought the one for his old house would work. He also wrote down Treyvon's name, thought hard about the number he knew he'd seen a million times on Treyvon's house by the front door, and wrote down what he could remember with the name of the street they'd lived on. He wasn't about to wait for his mother to get a mailbox in town. How would he be able to check it daily? He didn't know how far town was from the house but he knew there was no way his mother would allow him to ride his bike into town to check the mail by himself. He'd use the mailbox in front of the house. Maybe he could ask Treyvon to stop by his old house and get his posters and mail them to him.

~

Elijah didn't wait long before writing to Treyvon. His mother left him alone the next day to look for a job.

Before she left, she went over a bunch of new rules he'd have to follow. He wasn't allowed to answer the door, the phone, or leave the house when she wasn't home. He also wasn't allowed to eat anything that was supposed to be cooked. She showed him the breadbox, where the peanut butter and jam were, and told him if he got hungry to make himself a sandwich. But by no means was he to use the stove.

It was the first time Elijah had stayed home by himself and it was equal parts scary and thrilling. His mother told him it was something he might have to do frequently. She had to get a job, something she hadn't done since before she was married from what she told him. Not only did she not know anyone that could babysit him, she also didn't have the money to pay someone to watch him. She'd assured him it would be okay as long as he felt okay alone. They lived in the middle of nowhere with no neighbors. The likelihood of someone stopping at the house was extremely low and she'd left a list of emergency numbers on the fridge.

Now Elijah read the list of contacts, starting with the police, fire, EMS, Nana and Papa's new number, and ending with their old number before they'd moved. She hadn't put a name by their old number but he knew she only wanted him to call his father as a last resort, telling him it cost money to call long distance. He thought about calling Treyvon but assumed it would cost money to call him too and didn't want to make his mother mad. Mom had done nothing but talk about money the last couple of days and it didn't take much for him to realize it was something he didn't want to upset his mother over.

He took it upon himself to explore the house, starting with his mother's new room, which was his grandparents' old room. She didn't have anything he hadn't snooped through before. The rest of the house was the same. Most of the rooms were clear of anything other than some basic furniture. An old television sat in the living room and he gave up on watching anything after fiddling with it for ten minutes and only being able to get two channels to come in, neither airing anything of interest for a nine-year-old.

He finally turned his attention to the kitchen. The ceilings in the house were much higher than in his old house. He used a dining room chair as a step stool to open and search the top cupboards. There wasn't much in the way of food or cookery, but to his surprise, he discovered one of the drawers filled to the brim with all sorts of odds and ends. None of the items looked familiar and he thought it must've been stuff Nana and Papa left behind. He dug through the junk and was hit with a shock of delight when he discovered four dark blue stamps with a photo of a woman on them. The name Marianne Moore and the number twenty-five were printed above the woman's photo. He gleefully pocketed the stamps, grabbed a roll of scotch tape at the back of the drawer, and rushed to his room.

A notebook lay on his dresser, which he'd discovered in the closet earlier in the day. He snatched it up and feverishly wrote a letter to Treyvon. Elijah wrote about the house, how much he wanted to move back, and about his posters his mother had left behind. He asked Treyvon if there was any way he could go to his house and ask his dad for the posters and mail them to him. He was sure to include his new address before folding a clean sheet of paper and taping the edges to make a makeshift envelope. He stuffed the letter in the envelope, carefully printed Treyvon's address and his own before affixing a stamp.

His mother had told him not to go outside when he was home alone, but she'd also said no one would bother them "out in the sticks." He checked the window overlooking the drive and then the window facing the road. Everything was quiet and he didn't see any reason why he couldn't run out to the mailbox. There weren't even any cars on the road that ran in front of the house.

He bounded down the stairs and checked the drive once more, knowing his mother would be mad if she caught him outside, before throwing open the front door and running down the walkway. He was out of breath by the time he reached the rusty mailbox. This mailbox was much larger than the one at his old house. He grabbed the tab on the door and pulled. The door was stuck. He gave it a firm yank but it still didn't budge. The pole the box rested on wiggled in the ground as he pulled. He set the letter in the grass, grabbed the door tab the best he could with both hands and threw all his weight backward. The door broke free with a loud screech. The sudden release caused him to lose his balance. His hand slipped on the rusty door tab and the metal bit into his skin.

Elijah yelped and clutched his wounded hand. He cursed at the mailbox without thinking of the spanking his mother would give him if she heard him say such things (he'd learned them when his father was working on the car and smashed his hand last summer and from the movies he and Treyvon watched) and he kicked the loose pole the contraption rested on. He inspected the cut on his pointer finger and hissed as the blood dripped freely from the wound.

How am I gonna hide this from Mom? he thought.

"Damn it!" he shouted.

His shouting startled a bird resting in one of the pine trees and it tittered as it flew off.

Elijah looked at his wound. He needed to clean the cut and put a Band-Aid on it. He inspected the pull tab for the door and panicked. His mother had always warned him about rusty objects. She always talked about him getting tetanus. Elijah didn't know what tetanus was, but from the way his mother talked about it, he thought it was probably pretty bad. He needed to wash the tetanus out of the cut before his mom got home.

The letter to Treyvon still lay on the ground and Elijah noticed a few drops of blood had fallen on it.

"Oh no," he said.

He picked up the envelope with his good hand and wiped the paper on the grass, trying to wipe as much of the blood off as he could. Just as he was about to deposit the letter, he noticed a mass in the back of the mailbox. It looked like a clump of old grass but there was a divot in the center. It reminded him of a bird's nest. There wasn't any bird in the nest and he wondered how it had gotten inside of the mailbox. He decided to toss the envelope inside, dripping blood on the open door, and closed the lid before lifting the flag and running back inside to clean up his cut before his mother got home.

~

His mother didn't notice his bandaged finger at dinner. She was more focused on staring at her porkchop and pushing the mashed potatoes, applesauce, and peas around on her plate. She hadn't said much since she'd gotten home and he figured it was because she hadn't found a job.

Sometimes being an adult was something Elijah couldn't wait for because it meant being able to stay up late and do whatever you wanted whenever you wanted. But there were other times when adults made it look stressful and he really wasn't looking forward to that.

Elijah ate his dinner with gusto. He'd been so worried about the tetanus and getting it cleaned out of the cut on his finger, and whether or not his mother would be mad, that he'd forgotten to eat lunch. He was thankful his mother was distracted and hadn't noticed the three Band-Aids he'd wrapped around his finger to get the bleeding to stop. He was certain he'd cleaned up all the blood he'd dripped through the house but he was still nervous he might have missed something. He wasn't sure how his mother would react to the cut or the blood but he knew it wouldn't be good if she found out he'd left the house after he'd promised her he wouldn't.

Elijah dropped his bandaged hand under the table so his mother wouldn't see it. "Can I be excused?" he said.

His mother broke from her spell to look at his empty plate. "You must've been hungry."

He nodded. "Can I go outside and ride my bike?"

"Clean your plate ... and stay on the driveway or in the yard. Don't go on the road." She took a bite of her potatoes and stared at her porkchop.

Elijah jumped up from his chair and made quick work of cleaning his plate—soaking all three Band-Aids in the process—before setting the plate and utensils in the drying rack and bounding out the door. He jogged to the shed at the back of the property and retrieved his bike.

It was hard to pedal the bike through the overgrown grass and he wondered who was going to mow it. Maybe he'd get to mow it. He'd asked his dad several times that summer if he could mow their lawn, in hopes he'd get an allowance for doing so, but his dad had told him he was too young and he might get hurt. He didn't think his mother would be able to give him an allowance for mowing, but he didn't mind. Using the mower felt like a very adult thing to do and Elijah would be thrilled to do it.

His thighs burned from pedaling in the tall grass by the time he came upon the mailbox. He dropped his bike in the grass. The flag was still up on the mailbox. *The mailman will get it tomorrow,* he thought. But something was different about the mailbox. It appeared less delipidated. There wasn't as much rust as before. The pole the box was affixed to was straighter. He stared at the mailbox, trying to figure out if he was remembering it wrong. But no, the mailbox had less rust than before and the paint had more luster. Previously a dull black, now the paint was a little shiny.

He cautiously grabbed the tab to pull the door open. The door opened freely this time and without any sound. But he didn't expect what he found inside.

The letter was gone.

A flutter of panic rose in Elijah's chest. He quickly searched the ground, thinking the letter had somehow fallen out of the box. He didn't know how it would've fallen out but he'd been so flustered over his cut finger he may have missed it. But no, the letter wasn't anywhere.

He checked the mailbox again. The nest was still there but it looked different. The dried vegetation was a bit greener than before. There was something about the changes to the nest that made him feel uneasy. He wanted to remove it to see if somehow the letter had slipped underneath but he didn't want to touch it. Elijah searched the ground and retrieved a small tree branch near one of the pine trees. He used it to scrape the nest out of the mailbox and flung it in the grass. The nest broke apart when it hit the ground.

He checked the mailbox. The envelope wasn't inside. He turned his attention to the nest. He didn't see the envelope among the busted mass but did notice the nest was . . . wiggling. He timidly approached it with the branch still in his hand. Small white worms writhed within the busted pieces of the nest and the carcass of a dead bird was covered with them. He hadn't seen the bird before flinging the mess to the ground and wondered if the bird had been underneath the nest. The movement of the worms made his skin crawl. Elijah had heard of maggots before but he'd never seen them. He knew the letter wasn't in the mess and used the branch to hit pieces of the nest out into the road. He tossed the branch across the road and into the small ditch on the other side because it felt contaminated somehow and he didn't want it on the property anymore.

Elijah closed the mailbox's door and set the flag down. Maybe the mail had run when he was cleaning his cut and they'd forgot to put the flag down.

~

His mother woke him early the next morning for breakfast by calling for him from the bottom of the stairs. The sun was barely up and Elijah wasn't keen on the idea of getting up early during his summer vacation, but he dragged himself out of bed and downstairs before his mother could get short with him.

He found her sitting at the table with a half-eaten piece of toast and a cup of coffee when he entered the kitchen. Her hair was neatly pulled into a bun and she wore a plain dress with a touch of make-up. Make-up was something his mother rarely wore and was reserved for special occasions.

A newspaper was open on the table and his mother was circling want ads. A plate of scrambled eggs sat on the table in front of an empty chair. He took a seat and started his breakfast.

"Gotta go to the city today." She didn't look up from the paper as she sipped her coffee.

"There's a city?" He rubbed the crust from one eye and yawned.

"Yeah. It's about an hour drive. Not the most ideal but better than nothing." She screwed her face up in concentration before marking something in the newspaper. "I probably won't be back until dinner-time." She looked at him. "Ya gonna be okay by yourself, kiddo?"

He nodded and took a bite of his eggs.

She gave him a smile he knew wasn't real. "Only two more weeks until school starts, then you won't be home alone throughout the day. I'm tryin' to find something so I can be home in the evenin' with ya. But beggars can't be choosers."

Elijah wasn't sure why she was talking about begging. Was she begging for money every day? Were they that poor?

She said, "We'll go shopping for some new school clothes Saturday. Does that sound fun?"

He wanted to tell her it wouldn't be fun because he wanted to start the fourth grade with Treyvon. How could going to a new school and having to make new friends be fun? But he knew complaining would get him nowhere and it would only put her in a sour mood, and frankly, he was tired of being yelled at.

"Okay," he said.

Her smile became a bit more genuine. She picked up her piece of toast and glanced at the clock on the wall. "Oh," she said around the food. "I gotta get going. The early bird gets the worm." She rubbed her hands together and wiped the crumbs from them and onto her plate, stood, and cleared her side of the table.

Elijah was finishing his eggs when she retrieved her purse, reminded him to clean his plate, and hurried out the door. He was left with the sound of the ticking wall clock and the morning song of the birds and the distant sound of their car making its way down the gravel driveway.

He cleaned his plate before making his way to the bathroom to brush his teeth and then went upstairs to get dressed for the day.

He automatically headed for the window facing the road once he was in his room. He checked on the mailbox. The flag was up. *The mail must've ran early*, he thought.

The thought that a response from his letter would've taken more than a day's time to arrive never occurred to Elijah as he bounded down the stairs and out the front door. In his excitement, he hadn't stopped for shoes, and he nearly took a tumble on the dew slick grass when he stopped in front of the mailbox. He couldn't wait to read what Treyvon had written and hoped to find a package containing some of his things. The fact that the mailbox was in better condition than the day before didn't cross Elijah's mind as he ripped open the door. What he found inside made him shout in surprise and jump back.

A snake lay coiled up at the front of the box and he could see a piece of paper peeking out from under its scaly body. Elijah waited for the snake to rear its head or to slither out of the mailbox, but it didn't move. At first, he thought it might be asleep. But he was sure he could see its eyes and they were open. Elijah didn't know that snakes don't have a traditional eyelid and hence always appear to be awake, but the more he stared at the creature, the more he was certain there was something wrong with it. The snake's spine protruded beneath its skin and its body appeared deflated and dull, not shiny like the photos of snakes he'd seen in school. He knew some snakes could be poisonous but he wasn't sure which were and weren't and if any lived in the area.

After a few minutes of observing the snake and waiting for it to show any signs of life, he grabbed a stick lying on the ground by one of the pine trees, and poked the creature to try and roust it to leave the mailbox. The snake didn't react. It didn't react even after a couple more pointed jabs. Elijah realized the snake had expired. He wasn't sure how it had managed to get inside of the mailbox but he wanted the letter it was sitting on.

He used the stick to pull the dead snake from the mailbox, which proved more difficult than he anticipated. The snake was like a giant wet spaghetti noodle and was hard to maneuver without dropping it. But the snake was lighter than what he expected. Probably had to do with its emaciated appearance. He ended up retrieving a second stick and finagled the corpse out of the mailbox, carried it across the road, and managed to fling it into the ditch.

When he returned to the mailbox he realized the letter had fallen into the dewy grass. His heart rate picked up speed as he hurriedly retrieved the letter. There was no envelope. Just a piece of small paper folded in half. He opened the paper to find three words handwritten in a brownish substance: NEED MORE BLOOD.

Elijah was confused. It definitely wasn't Treyvon's handwriting. And he didn't understand the message. It didn't make any sense to him, and for some reason, it gave him gooseflesh. He checked the mailbox again, thinking the actual letter would still be inside, but found it empty. He wasn't sure if Treyvon was playing a joke on him but he didn't find it funny. Elijah balled up the paper and threw it as hard as he could across the road. He didn't bother closing the mailbox door before he stomped back up to the house.

~

Days passed before Elijah checked on the mailbox again. His mother had found a job working evenings, which meant he was alone when it grew dark outside, and his mother didn't get home until the sun had been down for several hours. The darkness made him nervous. The house was big and made bizarre sounds that, as much as he hated to admit it, frightened him when he was alone. The pops and ticks of the settling house sounded like footfalls sometimes. He never mentioned to his mother how much the house unnerved him once the sun set. His mother had to work and he didn't want her to worry about him while she was away.

He enjoyed the following weekend since his mother didn't have to work. They'd gone shopping for new school clothes and, as much as he hated the idea of starting a new school, he was starting to look forward to going back so he could get away from the house. Riding his bike up and down the driveway was growing old. There was nothing to build a ramp with and, even if there were, Elijah knew it wouldn't be the same without Treyvon.

Elijah wondered if Treyvon would ever respond to his letter and grew impatient. The Monday his mother returned to work in the afternoon, he penned another lengthy letter telling Treyvon how much he missed him. Once his mother left for work, he took it to the mailbox.

He was taken aback at the site of the mailbox. It was in pristine condition. The paint was glossy black and the flag was a vibrant red. Even the pole it sat upon looked new and didn't wobble anymore. Elijah was certain his mother hadn't replaced it because she would've told him or had him help. He wondered if the post office had replaced it.

He pulled the mailbox door open and the distinct odor of pennies wafted out. The box was empty and he deposited his freshly penned letter. He hoped Treyvon would answer this time. He only had a couple of stamps left and wasn't sure if his mother had any more.

After depositing the letter, Elijah entertained himself by trying to watch television. The channels that came in were staticky and the only thing on either channel was the news. There seemed to be a lot about some guy who said he was Jesus. Elijah didn't see what the huge deal was. The few times he'd attended Sunday school he'd been taught they should never question God. If the guy said he was Jesus, who had the right to challenge him?

He grew bored with the programming after a while and fell asleep on the sofa. When he awoke, the programming had changed to something a little more tolerable. Absentmindedly, he looked out the window at the mailbox. The flag was up. *I never heard the mailman*, he thought.

The sun was beginning to set. He debated on waiting until the next day to check it. Something about the encroaching darkness made him a little scared to go outside. But in the end, the desire to hear back from Treyvon was too strong. It wouldn't kill him to run out to the mailbox and check. *What if there's another snake in there?* he thought. *Or something worse?*

He swallowed his fear and forced himself to go outside. The closer he got to the mailbox the more an overwhelming sense of dread began to seep deep within him and into his bones. He didn't hesitate to yank open the mailbox door. In anticipation of discovering something awful inside, he jumped back when he flung the door open. But to his relief, there was only another folded slip of paper. No envelope. No package of posters. Just another piece of paper. He unfolded it and read it: PLEASE! NEED MORE BLOOD NOW!

The note made Elijah uneasy. He was beginning to think the mailman was trying to scare him and keep him from using it. Maybe the mailman was upset he had to get out of his vehicle to deal with their mail.

The door of the mailbox flipped shut on its own. The sudden movement startled Elijah. The door flipped open by itself to reveal another folded piece of paper.

Did I miss a second note?

He tentatively reached for the note but pulled his hand back, afraid the door could possibly shut on it. After all, it had just opened and closed on its own. The paper danced as if it were caught in an air current before it flew out of the mailbox and landed on the ground.

Elijah stretched his right leg toward the note and stepped on it before dragging it toward himself. He didn't trust the mailbox anymore. There was something definitely wrong with it and he was starting to believe Nana was right. The mailbox was cursed or possessed or something.

He opened the second slip of paper and read: DON'T BE AFRAID. I WILL DELIVER TREYVON'S LETTER AFTER YOU GIVE ME MORE BLOOD.

"What blood?" Elijah asked, staring at the open mailbox.

The mailbox lay still in response. A loud sound Elijah had never encountered before sounded from across the road. The noise was coming from the ditch. It was a deep and repetitive sound he knew had to belong to some sort of animal. The sun was almost below the horizon but he was compelled to investigate what was making the noise. He checked the road for any cars before crossing it. The sound ceased before he made it to the other side but started up again shortly after and he spotted the source of all the ruckus.

Elijah noticed the largest frog he'd ever encountered sitting among the weeds. The sound it made was foreign and funny to him and he was struck with the sudden thought that he needed to catch it and put it in the mailbox.

The mailbox needs more blood before I can get a letter from Treyvon.

The frog was slower and clumsier than the tiny toads he and Treyvon found near the downspout of his parents' garage. The frog leapt toward the tiny amount of water in the ditch but smacked into a cattail before landing on its back. Elijah was able to catch it as it struggled to flip itself over. The frog didn't struggle as he carried it across the road.

A feeling he couldn't explain told him to put the frog in the mailbox. He needed to feed it if he wanted to get any mail. And the mailbox wanted blood. This wasn't a prank Treyvon or the mailman were pulling on him. He was certain the bird he'd first found had been devoured by the mailbox. The snake had been sucked dry of any blood and that was the reason it looked emaciated and deflated. It was the only way he would be able to read Treyvon's letter. He placed the frog in the mailbox and shut the door.

He waited a minute. He was certain the door would pop open again on its own and Treyvon's letter would be inside. But nothing happened. The flag didn't rise either. The frog croaked loudly but didn't sound distressed. He cracked the door but was unable to see anything as it had grown near dark and he didn't like the idea of being outside the house once night fell.

Elijah relented to waiting another day and retreated to the house.

The next day he noticed the flag was up when he woke. After breakfast he retrieved his bike and road it through the grass to the mailbox. He opened the box, snatched up the folded piece of paper, and read it.

LET YOUR MOTHER CHECK THE MAIL.

The note confused him. "Where's my letter from Treyvon?"

As much as he wanted an answer from the mailbox, he knew it was ridiculous to expect it to actually speak. But he knew the mailbox understood him. He shut the door and waited a few seconds before opening it again, hoping it would prompt it to give him what he wanted. But the mailbox was empty. He didn't know why the mailbox wanted his mother to check the mail but he wasn't about to argue with it. He'd do whatever it asked as long as he could get a letter from Treyvon. He deposited the paper he'd read back into the mailbox and lifted the flag before riding his bike back to the house. Elijah dropped his bike by the door and hurried inside.

He found his mother sipping coffee in front of the television. She was still wearing her house coat.

"Mom," he said as he entered the living room. "The flag on the mailbox is up."

"Hmm." She was distracted by something on the television and had a difficult time prying her eyes from it to look at him. "The flag up means mail is going out."

"There's mail in the mailbox," he said. "You should check it."

"Oh, honey, it's probably junk mail. I told you, we don't use that box. The mailman must've gotten confused." She waited a beat. "If you know there's mail in it, why didn't you bring it in?"

"I think you should check it. What if it's not junk mail? What if Dad sent something?"

His mother flinched at the mention of his father. He could tell the thought of his dad sending her something excited her and she fought to keep her emotions in check. She said, "Why don't you check it?"

The lie came to him too easy. It was as if the mailbox was speaking through him. "I tried. The door is stuck."

"Stuck? Then how do you know there's mail in it?"

Elijah deflected her questions. "It looks rusty."

His mother mumbled as she rose to her feet. "Then how did the mailman get it open?"

Elijah shrugged. "Maybe he shut it too hard."

She sighed when she rose and made her way to the door. She slipped her feet out of her house slippers and into a pair of shoes she wore to mow the lawn. He'd hoped his mother would've allowed him to mow but she was still dead set against it. She told him he was too young and he might get hurt but promised she would teach him next summer.

Elijah watched his mother slip out the door, leaving the door open behind her. She was halfway to the mailbox when the phone rang. His mom stopped and turned to see him standing in the doorway watching her.

"Answer the phone, will ya?"

He sprinted to the kitchen to catch the phone before the answering machine switched on.

Out of breath, he said, "Hello?"

"Elijah, baby, how's my favorite grandson?"

"Hi, Nana. I'm your only grandson."

Nana chuckled on the other end. "Where's your mother? Is she at work all ready?"

"No." Elijah stretched the phone cord as far as he could, hoping it would make it to the doorway of the kitchen so he could watch his mother. "She's checking the mail and'll be back in a minute."

"The mail?" Nana's voice became stern. "I hope ya'll aren't using that mailbox. It's cursed, ya know."

He was trying to come up with a response when he heard his mother scream. Elijah had heard his mother scream once when she was damn mad, another time when she and his father were playing at the beach, and another time when a mouse managed to get inside of their house, but he had never heard his mother scream like this. It sounded like sheer terror and was cut short. He wondered if she'd found a snake in the mailbox too.

"What was that?" Nana asked. "Is everything okay there?"

"Yes. Everything is okay. I think Mom saw a snake."

"You be careful playing in that yard. There's copperheads in that area."

"Are copperheads poisonous?"

"You bet your little pu-tootie they are. You be careful. Ain't a hospital to be had within forty-five minutes of that house. Now, put your mama on."

"Okay. Hold on."

Elijah carefully let the phone receiver hang from the wall-mounted phone and rushed into the living room. His mother hadn't returned and the door was still open. He didn't see his mother anywhere in the front yard.

"Mom?"

He crossed the living room and stepped out the front door. He scanned the front yard and didn't see her. He jogged to the side of the house and checked the side yard and backyard. He called for her again but still got no answer. He shouted for his mother as he headed back toward the front of the house and scared a morning dove out of

42

one of the pine trees. Panic set in and he couldn't stop the tears from welling in his eyes.

"Mom! Where are you?"

The sound of metal scraping against metal drew his attention to the mailbox. The flag was still raised and the door was open. He ran to it and looked inside. One of his mother's shoes sat inside and it was covered in blood.

Elijah's breathing came fast and so did the tears. "Where's my mom? What did you do with her?" The mailbox didn't respond and he slapped the side of it. Sobs shook him between each word as he shouted, "Where's . . . my . . . mom?"

He grabbed the pole the mailbox was attached to and tried to shake it. He thought he might be able to wiggle it out of the ground and, if he did, he was going to throw it in the ditch. But the pole wouldn't budge. He kicked at it, hoping to knock it loose, but nothing happened. He grabbed the open door with both hands and pulled down on it as hard as he could. He wanted to rip the door off. He wanted to destroy the mailbox. But no matter how much he tried to rip the door from its hinges it wouldn't budge. He reached in the box, grabbed his mother's bloody shoe and found a note hidden beneath it. He knew it wasn't the original note he'd left there for his mother to discover and the unexpected reveal snapped him out of his fury. He didn't think twice about grabbing the note.

It happened so fast Elijah didn't have time to react. The metal of the mailbox screeched as the lid and opening stretched and grew, forming rows of jagged metal teeth, much like a shark. The door slammed shut on his forearm and the teeth sank deep into his skin. He screamed as the mailbox tightened its bite on his arm. The pain was unlike anything he'd experienced before, even worse than the time he wrecked his bike and had to get stitches because he hit his chin on the handlebars. He tried to pull his arm free but the mailbox clamped down harder. He heard and felt the bone break which sent him into a fresh wave of hysterics. Survival mode kicked in and Elijah yanked his arm as hard as he could. He tried not to look as the metal teeth sawed through the remaining flesh that was keeping his arm attached to his body.

He howled and jerked until his arm came free. He stared at the stump as blood squirted from the wound. The mailbox made an unfamiliar sound as it partially opened and closed its door in a movement that looked like laughter or possibly chewing. Elijah could see his severed hand and part of his forearm twitching inside the mailbox.

Elijah felt cold and shivered violently. There was so much racing through his mind all at once, and yet, he couldn't seem to concentrate on any one thing. *The phone*, he thought, *the emergency numbers*. His face felt numb and beads of sweat erupted all over his body. He trembled all over as he made his way back into the house. The sound of his own blood spattering on the floor as he crossed the kitchen toward the phone didn't faze him. Neither did the sound of Nana shouting for him and his mother from the phone's receiver as it dangled from the wall.

His remaining hand trembled, making it difficult to pick up the receiver. Once he got ahold of it, he lifted it to his ear. Nana's yelling hurt his eardrum.

"It's true." His voice came out as a harsh whisper.

"Elijah! What's going on there? Where's your mother?"

"I think . . . I think . . ."

"What? Speak up. I can't hear you."

Elijah was shaking uncontrollably and having a hard time holding on to the phone. He felt so cold and weak and fell to his knees. Vertigo kicked in and he was having a hard time staying awake.

"I think you were right, Nana. The mailbox is cursed."

He dropped the receiver before she responded. Nana was shouting but he couldn't understand what she was saying. He was tired and having a hard time keeping his eyes open. Elijah lay down on the kitchen floor and shut his eyes. It felt as if it took every ounce of his energy just to lay there, unmoving.

I'll just take a short nap, he thought, *and when I wake up, I'll call the police.*

IT CAME FROM THE SEA

"I DON'T KNOW ABOUT THIS," I said.

Teresa dropped my hand. Her shoulders slumped in a defeated manner. She turned to face me. Her expression was hard to read through her sunglasses but I could feel her disappointment. I readied myself for the bout of pleading.

"You promised," she said.

"I know. I know. I just . . ." I eyed the boats tied to the dock. They bobbed in the water lackadaisically. A gull cried out somewhere in the distance. "I don't know anything about boats and the sea is so endless . . . like the universe. You know, scientists don't even know everything that's in the ocean. It freaks me out."

"Jessie. Honey." Her disappointment dissolved. She rubbed my arm to comfort me. "I know what I'm doing. We won't stray far from the bay. I promise. We'll stay close enough for you to see land. Would that make you feel better?"

I made an uneasy sound. Teresa closed the gap between us and set her backpack on the ground. The sunlight made her blond hair shine. She leaned in to kiss me and wrapped her arms around my waist. She tasted like cherry ChapStick and smelled like sunscreen. We both wore shorts and tank tops over swimsuits and her skin against mine felt warmed by the sun. Warmth and lust flooded through me.

Teresa broke the kiss first. She said, "This is something I want to share with you. You promised you'd come with me when we met." She gave a small laugh. "I mean, we've met each other's parents. I think it's about time you met the sea." She half turned and waved down the dock. "I only sail half as much since you moved in. I feel like I should sell the damn thing."

I whined. "No. Don't do that. I don't want you to give up something because of me."

She took my hand and pouted. "Please try. I love you."

"I love you too," I responded automatically. I took a deep breath and let it out slowly, hoping it would calm my nerves. "All right . . . I hope I don't get seasick."

"Did you take the Dramamine?"

"Yes."

"You'll be fine." She lifted her backpack, slung it over one arm, and pulled on my hand. "Come on."

A sun-weathered man stood on the bow of his boat watching us with an intense curiosity as Teresa dragged me down the dock.

She stopped in front of a thirty-foot sailboat. Teresa jumped aboard first and then helped me. The boat bobbed unpredictably and walking was disorienting. She showed me around the deck, pointed at things, and rattled off the proper names for items I knew I would never remember. She made sure to show me the lifejackets and the emergency flares and explained how to use them because she knew it would put my mind at ease. Lastly she took me below deck to the cozy living quarters.

I was able to get around without stooping in the cabin but Teresa was taller and had to slightly bow. The boat had a tiny kitchen, a table with a bench, and a queen-size bed. The rocking of the boat was more disorienting below deck. Teresa emptied her backpack of the groceries and put the items in their respective places.

I flopped onto the bed and beckoned Teresa to join me.

"Oh no." She grabbed my arm and tried to pull me up. "The sea first."

"You're no fun."

I followed her back up the three steep stairs. I took a seat at the back of the boat. I didn't want to be an obstacle as she ran about to release the boat from the dock. She stopped by the wheel, inserted a key, and pressed some buttons. The motor started.

"I thought this was a sailboat," I said.

"It is. The motor makes it easier to maneuver out of the bay." She turned the wheel and the boat began to back away from the dock.

The boat didn't seem to bounce as much once it was in motion. As she steered through the bay I took the opportunity to enjoy the scenery. I avoided looking over the edge at the water and tried to put my fears aside. Once we were out of the bay the swells grew higher. The bounce of the boat became more jarring. I gripped a rail near my seat, terrified of being pitched over the side.

A boat passed us, a larger wave sweeping up to our boat. I thought, *This is it. I'm going to die.* Teresa stood at the wheel with her legs firmly planted. The muscles in her calves constricted as she balanced herself against the motion.

"This is scary!" I called over the noise of the motor and ocean.

Teresa looked at me over her shoulder. "It'll get better in a couple of minutes!"

"I hope so!"

A few more minutes into the open ocean and the swells calmed. Teresa slowed the boat and shut off the engine. She bustled around the deck, tying and untying ropes until the sails were lifted and in the correct position. I was amazed at how fast we traveled with only the aid of the wind. Once Teresa was satisfied with our position she lowered the sails and dropped the anchor. The shore was visible in the distance as she'd promised. I timidly gave in to the fear of the unknown and peered over the edge of the boat. I was shocked to find the water incredibly clear. I had imagined an endless void of blackness.

Teresa disappeared below deck and reappeared a few seconds later with two cans of beer. We stripped down to our swimsuits and sunned ourselves. Once Teresa finished her beer she decided to take a quick dip in the water to cool down.

I chose to watch her and thought it might set my mind at ease to see someone enter the water and exit unscathed. I stood at the ladder as she began to descend.

"Come on. It'll be fine." She grabbed my ankle playfully.

"I'm not ready." I held my hand to shield my eyes from the sun and tried to see if there were any fish near us. "I'm afraid if I felt a fish brush against me I'd panic and drown."

"All right. But you don't know what you're missing."

She bent down, grabbed a handful of water, and splashed me. She turned abruptly and dove into the water. She reappeared shortly, playfully splashed me, and disappeared below the surface. She continued this routine and I didn't mind the cooling effect of the water on my sun-warmed skin. I grew comfortable with the scenario, my fear of the sea abating some.

Teresa disappeared below the surface again but something was off this time. She was under longer than the previous times. The fear reared its ugly head and my heart skipped a beat as the microseconds collected and worry poisoned my thoughts. I called her name even though I was sure she wouldn't be able to hear me underwater. Panic coursed through my veins. I dropped to my knees by the ladder. I searched the water for her.

Suddenly she resurfaced a foot from the ladder, gasping for air, panic stricken. She latched onto a rung of the ladder and pulled herself up. I moved out of the way so she could climb aboard.

Still gasping for air, she shouted, "Something attacked me!"

"What?" My body vibrated with adrenaline.

Teresa dropped to her knees on the deck, fighting to regain her breath. She gripped her lower stomach and bent forward.

I knelt beside her and put my hand on her back. "Are you okay? What was it?"

"I don't know," she panted. "I thought I saw something but then an . . . eel attacked me."

"There're eels here?"

"I didn't think the water was shallow enough. I guess I was wrong. I don't know. It sorta looked like an eel or a snake or something. It was thinner than an eel. It was after my . . ."

Teresa sat back and looked at her crotch. A little blood ran down her thigh and mixed with the water on her body before dripping onto the deck.

"Oh my god!" I said. "We have to get you to a hospital!"

She stood and made her way to the living quarters below deck. I followed her in a state of panic. Her demeanor changed rapidly. Now stoic and calm, she entered the tiny bathroom and shut the door.

I stood outside the door and said, "I think we should go back."

I heard a cabinet open and close, followed by the unmistakable sound of tearing plastic.

"Teresa?"

"Give me a second."

"Are you hurt?"

"I started my period."

"Are you sure? It's a week early."

"What do you mean am I sure? I know what a period is."

Her retort stung. I took a step back from the door. She sounded angry and we'd never fought. The toilet flushed. I heard running water and the rattle of pills being shaken from a bottle. She opened the door, appearing peaked and tired.

"I'm sorry," I said, trying to dismantle an argument before it started. "I was worried."

She gave me a half smile. "It's okay." She popped the pills into her mouth and dry swallowed them. "I think I'm going to lie down for a few minutes." She rubbed her lower belly.

She always had cramps the first day of her cycle. I knew she wouldn't want to do anything until the aspirin did its job. I nodded and agreed to join her. She dried her hair with a towel, removed her swimsuit, and pulled on a pair of underwear before slipping into bed. I removed my suit and lay naked beside her. Sunlight shone on us from a skylight above the bed. I snuggled up to her. The rocking boat made it difficult for me to sleep but I eventually nodded off.

I woke an hour later to the sounds of cooking. I slipped out of bed. Teresa, wearing a T-shirt and shorts, was preparing hamburgers on a single electric burner.

She said, "Food's almost done."

"What time is it?" I dug through my bag and pulled some clothes on.

"Eight o'clock." She flipped the burgers.

I retrieved condiments from the mini fridge and sat at the table. Two paper plates sat on the counter. Each plate held a bun. Only one bun had a slice of tomato and lettuce on it. Teresa scooped up the burgers and sat them on the buns. She brought both plates to the table and sat the one with tomato and lettuce in front of me.

"Thank you," I said.

Teresa put the top bun on her burger, lifted it, and took a bite. I added ketchup and mustard to mine.

I said, "You don't want anything on yours?"

She spoke around a full mouth. "No."

I took a bite and realized mine was rare. I wasn't a fan of rare burgers. I preferred medium-well. Teresa swallowed and took another bite. A mixture of blood and grease splattered on her plate. I'd never known Teresa to eat a burger any other way than well-done. She'd previously given me a hard time, saying medium-well was barbaric.

I said, "You're eating a rare burger?"

She shrugged and continued chewing. Her demeanor was guarded and something felt wrong. I wrote it off to her starting her period even though she wasn't one to suffer irritability or mood swings during her cycle. I knew I would be agitated if I'd planned a getaway for the two of us and my period decided to come early and became an obstacle for intimacy. We finished our dinner in silence.

After dinner we sat on the deck and watched the sunset. Teresa was distant and avoidant of conversation. She stared at the water and I took the opportunity to read while there was still daylight. A few boats passed in the distance, exiting and entering the bay. When the sun slipped over the horizon the lights on the shore became more prominent. Teresa illuminated the outside of the boat so other boats were aware of our presence. The boat's lights were blue and cast eerie shadows. We drank a few more beers and I watched the other boats maneuver in the night to take my mind off the pitch-black and endless appearance of the sea. Eventually we retired for the night. I hoped a good night's sleep would improve Teresa's mood.

~

Teresa woke me from a dreamless sleep. The blue lights barely filtered through the skylight. It took me a few sleepy and alcohol-fueled seconds to realize where I was and what was happening.

Teresa was spooning me. We'd gone to bed in our underwear and the skin of her bare breasts was cool against my back. Her chilly hand wandered into my underwear. She began to work her finger in and out of my vagina.

"Teresa?" I said.

"Hmm."

She removed her finger from inside me and began to rub my clit. The heat of my arousal cleared the sleep and lingering alcohol from my mind. She kissed the back of my neck and licked my shoulder. Her tongue was as cool as her touch. Goosebumps rose on my skin.

I whispered, "Your period . . ."

An orgasm began to build within me. I arched my back and pressed my buttocks into her crotch. She ground her pubis into me. My breathing became loud and the heat of my growing orgasm caused me to break out in a thin layer of sweat.

Teresa whispered, "It was a false alarm." Her words were hoarse and slurred.

The term "false alarm" meant she had spotted but didn't actually start her period. I thought there was a lot of blood for it to be a false alarm but put it out of my mind.

I gave myself over to the orgasm and bucked with each wave of pleasure as Teresa continued to coax my clit. She made an agreeable sound and delivered more kisses to my neck and shoulder. Once my orgasm had subsided I rolled over to face her.

The faint blue light cast dark shadows and made everything barely visible. Teresa's lips appeared dark. I tried to deliver a kiss but she placed her hands on my shoulders and applied a gentle downward pressure, letting me know what she wanted. I kissed her collarbone and trailed my lips to one of her taut nipples. Her skin was clammy and I wondered if she was running a fever or if it was the effect of the night ocean air. I sucked and licked her nipple while gently pinching the other. Her skin tasted salty. She cooed and tried to grind her pubis into me before grabbing my hair and guiding me farther down her body. I removed her panties and she spread her legs to reveal her shaved but stubbly pussy. She smelled like the ocean. I slipped my hands under her thighs, grabbed her hips, and began to lick her clit. She moaned and held the back of my head while I worked. I slipped two fingers inside of her wet vagina and began to coax her G-spot while licking her clit. She removed her hand from the back of my head and I looked up at her to see her pinching her own nipples and staring at me with an angry expression. Her look gave me pause. My fingers hit an obstruction inside of her, followed by a sharp prick to the fingertips.

I yelped, withdrew my hand from inside her, and shot up to a kneeling position. I examined my fingers in the scant light. They glistened with Teresa's juices. A darker liquid ran down my hand from the tips of my two wounded fingers.

Teresa sat up without a word. I slipped out of bed and checked my hip on the corner of the kitchen table before fumbling with the light switch by the kitchenette. I squinted against the sudden brightness. I examined my fingers over the sink. Two crescent shaped slits marked either side of each finger. It appeared they'd been pinched by something with enough force to make a clean cut in the skin.

Teresa had slipped out of bed and now stood with her feet planted far from each other at the foot of the bed, fifteen feet from me.

"Something cut me," I said.

I turned my attention to Teresa. In my confused state, it took a few seconds to register her condition. Her skin was a sickly shade of gray and her eyes had become milky. Her lips were crimson and blood dripped down her chin. A black protuberance as long as her torso extended from her vagina. Blood ran down her thighs and a serpent-like thing swayed listlessly back and forth from her vagina. The thing stopped moving and fixed its white eyes on me.

"Teresa?" I whimpered. I gripped the counter and began to shake.

She took a clumsy step. Her voice was thick and didn't belong to her. More blood leaked from her mouth when she spoke. "It's okay." Her tongue was black and pointed and covered in blood. "It doesn't hurt." The creature protruding from her vagina inclined its head toward me and I knew the tip of its tail was acting as her tongue. She took another step toward me.

I fumbled on the counter for something to protect myself with and found nothing. Teresa took another slow step toward me and I wrenched open a kitchen drawer. The drawer came free from the cabinet, sending cooking utensils clattering onto the floor. I spotted a butcher knife and crouched to snatch it up. I stayed on my haunches and pointed the knife at Teresa who'd crossed half the distance between us. She stopped. The creature regarded me with curiosity.

My voice quivered and broke. "Stay away from me!" Tears threatened to spill from my eyes.

I stood and began to reach for the radio mounted on the wall beside the sink. I didn't know how to use it but I had to try. Even a squawk of help would draw attention.

The serpent slid from within Teresa's lifeless body and she crumbled to the floor before I could manage to call for help. A sob of grief escaped me but there was no time. The serpent quickly crossed the distance between us and encircled my leg. I caught it behind its head with my free hand and stopped it six inches from my crotch. I was thankful I had on underwear but knew the material wouldn't stop it if it got loose. Teresa's swimsuit hadn't stopped it. The thing flailed its head back and forth, snapping its jaws and trying to bite me. It was cold and slimy with Teresa's blood. Up close I could see its gills.

I struggled to keep a hold on the creature and cut it with the butcher knife. It kept squirming and repositioning itself around my leg. I sliced wildly, missed it, and cut my thigh. I screamed in frustration and my grip slipped an inch. The end of the creature was coiled around my ankle and the tip of its tail lay on the ground between my feet. Its underbelly was exposed toward the tip of its tail and I could see a slit in its skin. I assumed it was either its anus or sex. The creature slipped more, gaining ground. Another inch and the thing would be able to twist and bite my wrist. In a last desperate attempt I lifted my free leg and brought my heel down as hard as I could on the spot I thought might be vulnerable.

Pain shot up my calf from the impact. The creature screeched, backed out of my hold effortlessly, and let go of my leg. It flopped around wildly on the floor. I didn't wait for it to regain itself.

I ran up the steps for the door, almost fell when I pulled it inward, and slammed it behind me. I peered through the window on the top half of the door and didn't see the creature. My hand lay on the horizontal lever handle and I felt it move. I gripped the handle and pulled the door while trying to see what was happening on the other side.

The creature had coiled itself around the handle and was trying to use its weight to open the door.

I held the door handle and began to search the immediate area for a solution. The lighting was terrible. I spotted a dark coil a few feet away, shrieked, and started kicking in its direction, thinking it was another one of the snake-things and it had slithered out of the sea. It took a few seconds for me to realize the motionless coil was a rope.

At a loss, I checked back through the window to find the creature staring at me through the glass. I knew I had to either kill it or get off the boat. For the moment, I had it trapped. If I could keep it contained long enough maybe I could figure out how to steer the boat back to the shore.

I held the doorknob and extended my leg toward the rope. Using my foot I managed to get hold of the rope, pull it toward me, and find the end. I tied the rope around the door handle, held it taut, and started to back away.

The creature reared back and slammed its head into the window. With enough force, the glass would break. I knew my time was limited.

I kept the rope taut and ran toward the side railing. The boat swayed with the ocean. I slipped, my momentum almost launching me over the side. There were smears of something dark on the deck and I knew the self-inflicted knife wound needed staunching soon.

I secured the rope to the rail. The creature banged rhythmically against the glass as I worked. When I was done with the rope I stumbled over to the wheel.

Panic had taken hold of me and my hands shook uncontrollably. I tried to calm myself and think. I knew I had to lift the anchor first. I ran toward the front of the boat and tried to remember what Teresa had done. She had tied a length of rope around the chain to the anchor and attached it to the boat. I struggled with the knots and heard a familiar sound in the distance.

A set of lights bounced rhythmically along the water in the

direction of the bay. By the sound of its engine I could tell it was a speed boat. I immediately stopped what I was doing and turned to run toward the wheel. I slipped on some of my own blood, fell, and hit my chin on the deck. My teeth slammed against each other and sparks of pain illuminated my vision. I forced myself to get up. I couldn't stop, because if I did, I would end up dead like Teresa. My heart ached, knowing she was gone.

I held the railing and rushed back to the wheel. It dawned on me that the sound of the creature banging its head on the window had ceased. There were smears of blood on the intact window. The thing had probably knocked itself unconscious.

I threw open the bench seat near the wheel and retrieved the orange flare gun box. I tried to remember how Teresa said it worked. The contents of the box spilled onto the deck when I opened it upside down.

The other boat was picking up speed and would pass in less than a minute. I grabbed the comically fat gun and one of the shells rolling around on the deck. I tried to force the gun open. While fumbling with it I pulled the hammer. The gun opened.

A loud clack drew my attention to the cabin door. The thing had reappeared and was now hammering the window with a butter knife it held in its mouth.

I said, "You've got to be fucking kidding me."

Clack! The tip of the knife put a crack in the window.

Time was up. I had to get off the boat.

I rammed the flare in the gun and snapped it shut. I lifted the gun into the air and pulled the trigger. The flare shot into the night sky, sputtering and flashing. Something deep inside me screamed triumphantly but a rational part said it didn't matter. The boat wouldn't make it. I was going to die. Maybe that was better. I would be with Teresa. I only wished the death wouldn't hurt.

Clack!

The sound of the boat's motor dropped an octave as it slowed and changed course. The vehicle made a beeline toward me. I watched the other boat as the smack of metal on glass continued behind me. The boat was fast but oddly felt as if it were moving in slow motion.

There was nothing I could do but wait to see who made it first. Through the panic of impending death some of my senses came back. I was still holding the flare gun. I flipped the hammer, dumped the spent shell, and dropped to the deck in search of another. I found one rolling back and forth by the wheel and reloaded.

The engine from the approaching boat stopped and it continued to drift toward me.

Another clack produced the sound of breaking glass. The creature had chipped a small hole in the glass at the bottom of the window frame but it wasn't big enough for it to pass through.

"Ahoy!" someone shouted in the distance. "Is everything okay?"

The other boat drifted fifty feet away and was only half the size of Teresa's. The lighting on their craft was yellow and bright. A portly man gripped the railing. A short chubby woman stood beside him. They were both clad in matching windbreakers. I reflexively covered my naked breasts with one arm.

The creature hit the glass again.

I shouted, "I'm being attacked by an animal!" I sobbed. "It killed my girlfriend! Please get me off this boat!"

The man leapt toward the wheel of his boat.

The woman shouted, "Are you a good swimmer?"

Tears sprang from my eyes as the fear of the ocean came crashing back. "I don't want to get in the water! That's where it came from!"

The other boat's engine roared to life and the craft began to close the distance. Another piece of glass fell and shattered. I turned to spot the creature dropping the knife. It cautiously started through the hole it had created. I screamed, pointed the flare gun at the creature, and pulled the trigger. The flare embedded into the door a foot below the window. The creature recoiled from the flare and screeched.

The boat lurched beneath my feet, followed by a crunching noise.

I grabbed the railing to keep from falling.

"Bill!" the woman shouted. "You'll sink us both!"

Our boats were touching.

The creature was making its way out and around the flare. I threw the gun at the creature and scrambled over and onto the other boat. The woman had made her way to me. She helped me down onto the deck.

"Go! Go! Go!" I shouted. "Before it gets on your boat!"

"Bill!" the woman shouted.

The boat roared and shot forward. The woman and I fell to the deck. The sound of the two boats scraping against each other briefly filled the night and I thought we might sink.

The sound stopped and we were speeding away.

I sat up and leaned against a bench. The woman beside me did the same, pulling off her windbreaker and wrapping it around me. I began to sob uncontrollably. The boat's speed stabilized enough for us to stand.

The woman said, "We'll get you back to land."

I nodded at her. I searched for the sailboat in the distance and spotted the ghostly blue light. But there was something else about the boat. A large shadow, barely perceptible against the night sky, hung over the boat. The woman followed my gaze. I blinked and tried to decipher what I was seeing. A large serpentine entity protruded from the ocean. Its head hovered a hundred feet above the boat.

"What is that?" the woman said. She yelled at the man, "Look at that!" She pointed at the boat. "What is it?"

The man pulled a lever by the wheel and his boat slowed. He squinted into the night at the other craft. The shadow suddenly darted downward and crashed across the middle of Teresa's boat. The craft buckled and split. The man killed the engine of his boat and the three of us watched as Teresa, the boat that was her second love, and whatever had taken her life, bobbed and twisted and slowly sank into the sea.

SWIPE LEFT

THE WOMAN SITTING BESIDE ME at the bar stirred her cocktail lackadaisically with the thin black straw it was served with. She stared at a small bit of mirror peeking out from behind the rows of liquor bottles where I assumed she could see her reflection. She said, "So, Jon, what do you do?"

I was glad she was initiating the obvious round of questions. Quite frankly, this part of the date bored me to tears. Especially since we both knew why we were here and pussyfooting around made me antsy.

I'd only met Tonya five minutes prior but her unenthusiastic demeanor made it apparent she wasn't really into me. And in return I'd wanted to leave as soon as I arrived. The moment we shook hands I got the feeling our meeting was going to be a huge waste of time. I wasn't sure what the protocol was for ditching someone you'd met online but I wished more people would be forthright in telling the other person they just weren't into them the moment they laid eyes on them. I knew I wasn't the most attractive or engaging guy but I wasn't downright repulsive and that was the vibe Tonya was throwing off. Maybe, since I was over thirty, I could've done better than the five-year-old snapshot I'd used for a profile photo. Maybe she thought I was catfishing. The thought was ridiculous and almost made me laugh. If I were catfishing I would've filled out the questionnaire to make me look more successful or more interesting. No sense in trying to sugarcoat what everyone on the site was looking for . . . a one-night stand.

Tonya's and my introduction had been awkward. And I was certain that was an understatement. I didn't think any couple's meeting in a bar after a short conversation on Tinder went all that smoothly. I'd never been too good at casual conversation. The whole situation was inevitably going to end in disappointment for one or the other of us, possibly both. The more Tonya gave me the cold shoulder the more I thought we would both end up going home frustrated and disappointed.

"I'm a customer service representative," I said.

She didn't acknowledge me in any way, only stirred her drink and stared at her reflection.

I added, "I work from home so I don't get to meet people very often."

She finally turned on her stool and looked at me with a touch of warmth. "No friends?" She genuinely seemed slightly interested. Or maybe I was misreading her. Now she at least seemed interested in something other than her reflection.

"I've sorta been a loner my whole life. Probably for the best." *Why were we having this conversation?* I thought. *It's all superfluous and a time suck. We both know why we're here. She either wants to fuck me or she doesn't.*

"Why's that?" she said and took a sip of her drink.

The bartender stopped to ask if we needed anything. I lifted my beer to show him only the top quarter of the pint was missing. He nodded and moved toward the other end of the bar where another couple who seemed to enjoy each other's company were talking.

I answered Tonya, "No siblings and both of my parents died in a car accident a few years back. I never kept in contact with any extended family. They all seemed like horrible people anyway."

"I'm sorry," she said. "About your parents. Who needs horrible people in their lives?"

Her eyes lit up, which I found peculiar for such a morbid disclosure on my part. I took another drink of my beer.

She said, "And unlucky in love?" She raised her glass to toast me.

I clinked my glass against hers. "Aren't we all?"

She smiled for the first time since we'd met and it appeared forced and artificial. The smile didn't reach her eyes. I wondered if she was trying to hide her age. You could really tell a person's age when they smiled. Crow's feet. Laugh lines. They were hard to disguise without either money for plastic surgery or some tiny bottle of age elixir that cost more than my monthly rent. She took a long drink from her glass.

"You?" I said. "How 'bout you? What do you do? Do you have siblings? Parents?" I hesitated. "Children?"

If I hadn't been staring at her I would have missed the slightest reaction at the last question. My first thought was maybe she wanted children and couldn't have any. Or maybe she hated children. Who knew anymore what anyone really wanted out of life? I'd met more people who were inclined to stay single and asexual the rest of their lives. Sleeping in and living off gas station snacks like a perpetual teenager that bitched about how unfair life was.

"I'm a paralegal," she said. She looked at her drink and her expression dimmed. "And I don't have anyone." She turned back to me and smiled, a forced smile again, and said, "There just isn't any time. My job keeps me pretty busy."

I nodded. "I know the feeling." I added, "We'd both make perfect victims."

Her expression turned worried. "What do you mean?"

I backpedaled. "I'm sorry. I'm not a psychopath or anything. I didn't mean anything by it. It's just . . . I used to work in an office and

I once told a coworker about my situation. You know . . . no family or close friends. He said I'd make the perfect victim. No family or friends means you could be gone for a while before anyone ever noticed. *If* they ever noticed."

"Oh." She gave a half-hearted laugh. "I see. I guess I never thought of that."

Another beat of silence passed between us and she drained the last of her drink before motioning to the bartender for another. The night wasn't going to go any quicker after putting my foot in my mouth and I thought I should at least try to keep up with her. I hurriedly drank my beer before the bartender made his way back over to us and ordered another round for the both of us.

Neither of us spoke while our drinks were being served and each second of silence was making the situation unbearable. Tonya began to stare at her reflection again. And I had to refrain from asking her if she was still even remotely interested in fucking tonight.

Instead I tried to fill the void of awkwardness by saying, "You look pretty." I took another long drink of my beer.

She gave her reflection a half-hearted smile. She sat up straighter. Her shirt was low-cut and it appeared she was trying to accentuate her assets. Tonya lifted her glass and said, "Thank you," before downing her entire drink. She set her glass down gently on the bar top and turned to me. "Let's get out of here and go back to my place."

There it was.

I motioned for the bartender and chugged the last of my beer. I asked for him to charge the total to the debit card he was holding hostage and glanced at Tonya's reflection in the mirror. I noticed a growing dark spot on her shirt by her nipple.

I didn't want her to think I was staring at her chest so I turned to watch the bartender before I said, "I think you might've spilled some of your drink on your shirt." In my periphery I spotted her checking her reflection.

"Shit," she mumbled under her breath. "Be right back."

"I'll be here," I said.

She grabbed her purse and rushed toward the hall to the ladies' room. It wasn't until she was out of my sight that I worried she'd found a way to bail on me. If I had to be honest, I wouldn't blame her. The bartender was more interested in me than Tonya was but I guess that mainly had to do with the overpriced drinks.

At least five minutes passed and I began contemplating leaving. Tonya had most likely slipped out a back door on the way to the ladies' room. I was an idiot to think she wanted anything more from me than a few free drinks. Just when I was about to leave she reappeared from the darkened hallway. She didn't look happy and I refused to look at the now larger dark spot on her shirt.

"Everything okay?" I asked.

"Let's go," she said as she passed me.

She didn't bother stopping as she made her way toward the door. Maybe she was more eager than I'd originally thought.

I hailed a cab once we were outside and Tonya gave the driver her address. The cab ride was filled with more of the same uncomfortable silence. Eventually she shot me a coy smile that didn't seem genuine and turned her attention to the back of the driver's head.

I struggled with whether or not I should try to touch her or kiss her. I wasn't embarrassed to admit I had a fragile ego and wanted the woman to make the first move. I wanted to feel wanted or desired. And I was terribly afraid of rejection and failure. I could never be sure, especially with Tonya, if a woman was actually into me or not. The last thing I wanted was to offend them, or assume the night was going to end in sex, only to find out they wanted something different, even though Tonya had invited me back to her place. She'd never actually said "I want to have sex with you" and she seemed friendlier while chatting online than in person. Even if the whole night had begun on a sleazy dating website, progressed to both of us meeting at a bar, and she had initiated our leaving and going back to her place together, I wasn't a hundred percent sure how the night was going to end. I'd met a few women who, despite going through all the actions, had only wanted to talk and wanted much more than a onetime fling. I was much more comfortable with casual sex. That was sort of the thrill of online dating, the anticipation. The unknown. Falling in lust over and over.

"Here," she said and pointed to a small house.

My mind was so wrapped around whether or not I should take her hand or touch her thigh that I didn't realize we'd entered a meticulously landscaped suburb. The driver pulled into the driveway of the house. In the dark the place looked like it was either a light blue or gray. It was difficult to tell as the street lighting was poor, there were no security lights on outside the house, and no lights were on anywhere inside the house.

Tonya exited the car and made her way to the front porch while I paid the driver with my debit card. Once I was out of the car my nerves started to kick clear the two beers from my head. Even in the dark Tonya's hourglass silhouette was something to behold and my heart rate picked up.

I stood by as she fumbled with her keys on the dark stoop and unlocked the door. As the door opened, a peculiar smell hit me and for some reason it brought back memories of my mom's funeral. Tonya's house smelled of something floral and some sort of chemical preservative and there was a hint of sour milk.

Her shoes clicked against the hardwood floor as she stepped in and flipped a light switch near the door. The light cast a warm yellow glow over a scrupulously clean home. The place was decorated in such a way that it looked as though it could be a Pier 1 showroom. Tonya switched on lights as she made her way through the house. I followed her and peered into the dining room. There was a large bouquet of roses as the center piece on the table and I now understood the strong floral scent.

She showed me to the living area arranged with overstuffed furniture and wicker and gold bric-a-brac on white shelves, along with more than a few pieces of taxidermy.

"Have a seat," she said. "I'm gonna get a drink. Would you like something?"

I sat on the sofa. "Sure."

"Beer? Wine? Cocktail?"

"Beer is fine. Thanks."

She nodded before exiting to the kitchen. I studied the items on her shelves. There were no books. Just overpriced garbage with no sentimental or artistic value that people buy to fill some sort of void I could never understand. And the taxidermy looked bad. It was either old and uncared for or done by an amateur. There were gold framed photos of safe landscapes that reminded me of bad hotel art hung on the walls. Her house actually looked like a skewed and nightmarish version of a display house the more I paid attention to it, and I wasn't sure if it was the beer thinking for me, but it started to give me the creeps when I spotted a photo of a baby. I couldn't be sure if the lighting was playing tricks on my eyes but something didn't look right about the infant and I didn't want to get up to look at the photo and have Tonya catch me. I was certain that would only end in an unwanted conversation.

I started to wonder if coming here was a bad idea. I should've invited her to my place. But the thought of having someone in my house who may end up being mentally unbalanced and who may decide they didn't need to leave made me hesitant to invite any dates over.

Tonya returned with a beaming smile. She appeared genuinely happy this time. Her eyes gleamed as she handed me a bottle of beer. She pulled two coasters from a drawer in the coffee table and dropped both on the tabletop on either side of a gold embossed photo album before she sat in a chair opposite the sofa. Maybe sex wasn't in the cards tonight. I would think, if she did want to fuck, she'd have taken a seat next to me. Maybe she was trying to play hard to get.

She lifted her large glass to me before taking a drink. It appeared she was drinking water or possibly vodka. If the glass she was drinking from—which appeared it could hold nearly a pint and a half—happened to be filled with vodka, I do believe Tonya was a boozehound. I don't know anyone who could drink that much hard liquor in one sitting and not end up in the hospital.

She smiled coyly at me before downing more of her drink. I followed her lead and drank half of my beer, thinking maybe she was settling her nerves.

I looked around the room again. "You have some interesting taxidermy."

"Do you like it?"

I shrugged. I eyed what I thought was a crow and drank the rest of my beer. "I don't know how I feel about dead animals as decoration. Sort of creepy."

Her face fell.

There I went, putting my foot in my mouth again.

She said, "It's an excellent way to preserve something so you can admire it forever."

I didn't respond. I got the feeling I'd offended her. And now I knew the night wasn't going to end well.

Tonya sat her drink down and stood abruptly. She walked over to the shelf I'd been eying and grabbed the crow. She sat beside me on the sofa and began to turn it over in her hands, scrutinizing the entire thing. She offered it to me and I took it reluctantly. It was hard and unmoving and nothing about it appeared natural or alive up close. I handed it back to her and she sat it on the coffee table so the thing could stare directly at us.

I suddenly began to feel slightly dizzy. I went to take another drink of my beer but remembered once I'd lifted the bottle it was empty. I sat the bottle down clumsily on the coffee table. My hearing grew muffled and the room began to spin a little.

"Can I . . ." My tongue felt thick and sluggish. "Can I get a drink of wa . . . ter?"

She chuckled and put her hand on my thigh. "You'll be fine in a few more minutes."

"Wha . . ." I struggled to process what she meant. "I ung fe goo nnh." I tried to lift my hand to my forehead but my arm didn't seem to have the strength to do what I wanted it to. *Am I having a stroke? What is happening? Something is wrong.* My eyes were heavy and I struggled to turn my head toward Tonya.

She looked me up and down with an excited expression as my body began to go slack. I tried to grab at anything to keep from falling as I sank into the sofa in slow motion. My arms felt like they were made of lead and flopped like fish out of water.

Tonya patted my thigh. "There we go," she said.

She stood up and disappeared down a hall just past the kitchen. There was the sound of a door opening and, shortly after, Tonya began cooing. All of the sound was muffled and my hearing was cutting in and out. It was difficult to hear what she was saying. I tried to call out but my mouth was no longer functioning. I'd fallen on the sofa so I was partially lying and facing the coffee table. I tried my hardest to move but nothing would cooperate. The night wasn't going to end well unless Tonya had some sort of dead fuck fetish because it was obvious she'd drugged me.

Although they were muffled I could make out footfalls. I tried to turn my head and resorted to turning my eyes instead to try and see down the hallway. It was just out of my line of sight and the strain made my eyes twitch and hurt. Tonya reappeared with a tall wooden contraption.

My mind was in such a muddied state that it took a few seconds to comprehend what she sat beside the chair across from the sofa . . . an old-fashioned highchair. In the contraption sat a tiny mottled and deformed baby. Its unusually blue eyes glistened with the artificiality of glass or something that wasn't its actual eyes. As the image of the infant sank in, my lungs wanted to expand and fill with a terrified scream but they now felt as though they were cast in cement. What did come to me was crystal-clear hearing instead.

Tonya lifted the infant from the highchair and cradled it in her arms as if it were alive and began to nuzzle the abomination. She sat in the chair and ran her fingertip along its closed lips and cooed, "Are you hungry? I bet you are. Mommy's been gone for a while, hasn't she?" She pulled down the lowcut neck of her shirt to expose a nursing bra and unfasted the cup to expose her engorged breast with thick blue veins close to the skin's surface. She placed her nipple against the taxidermized infant's lips and began to squeeze her breast so milk shot onto its closed mouth and spilled over its clothing before spattering on the floor.

"Ugnth," I weakly managed.

She turned her attention to me as if she'd forgotten I was there. She held the infant as if it were really nursing and leaned to one side. Tonya retrieved her phone from her back pocket and hit a button and stared at the screen. She sighed with an air of aggravation before dropping the phone on the coffee table. She used her shirt to wipe the baby's mouth, pulled her bra and top back into the correct position, and sat the infant back in the highchair. She approached me and began rummaging around in my pockets, retrieving my wallet and cellphone. She dropped my phone on the coffee table and I stared at it as if my mind could somehow will it to call 911. Tonya began to rifle through my wallet. She pulled every card, note, and currency from their worn spaces and dropped them on the coffee table also. She barked a laugh once she withdrew the condom I'd stashed there before leaving to meet her.

"Not how you planned the night ending, huh?" she said with a twisted grin as she waved the condom in my face.

She tossed the prophylactic over her shoulder and grabbed my belt and unfastened it. I tried to protest but ended up gurgling. She yanked at my jeans and underwear roughly to expose my flaccid penis.

"Aw, is he scared?" she taunted.

She grabbed my penis and began to roughly tug on it. As much as I tried to fight it my body began to respond to her touch. It'd been a while since I'd been touched by a woman and I started to think that being drugged and fucked by a crazy person wasn't too terrible. But deep down I knew that wasn't the reason she'd drugged me.

Tonya studied my semi-erect penis as if it were a riddle. She lifted my shirt to my neck and pinched her lip in thought before grabbing my arm and roughly pulling me into a proper sitting position. The room began to swim again and I felt nauseated. I wondered what she would do if I vomited. I wondered if I would choke on my vomit since I was unable to will any part of my body to do what I wanted.

She took a few steps back and scrutinized me. "I guess sitting is probably the best position. What do you think?" The expectant expression on her face almost made her appear like an innocent child. She pursed her lips. "Hmm."

She kicked off her shoes and unfastened her jeans before sliding them and her underwear off. She straddled me and grabbed my penis, which had gone completely soft, to position me for sex. I squeezed my eyes shut but was forced to open them when I was hit with a wave of vertigo.

"I don't know," she said close to my face. Her breath smelled like fruit juice and the tang of alcohol. "Lying down would be best. But then you'll always be standing when you're not in bed. And I'll have to make a base to keep you upright."

I managed to make my shoulder twitch. I tried to tell her to get off me but all that came out was, "Nugf."

"Not enough?" she said. "I know. I'll get more in a second."

She stood and retrieved the baby. She sat the thing next to me and scrutinized the two of us and began to tear up. "We're going to make the perfect family. Here . . ." She dashed to a shelf and grabbed a polaroid camera and snapped a couple photos of me with the baby, even though my dick was still exposed. "I'm gonna add it to my photo album." She fanned one of the photos before showing it to the baby.

"Look, Daddy's first day home." She tossed the photo on the coffee table.

She picked up the photo album and sat on the coffee table. She opened it and flipped through a few pages before turning it to show me a photograph of her, sweaty and lying in a hospital bed, cradling the obviously fresh-born child sitting beside me. It was evident by its pallor the poor thing had been stillborn and I was certain, if I was able to turn my head to look at the baby photo I'd seen on the wall, I would now realize what was wrong with the photo: Its subject was deceased.

"Isn't he beautiful?" She turned the album back around and began turning the pages slowly. She wept openly, lost in reminiscence.

As horrifying as the whole situation was, I really wished I could've asked her how she managed to steal the dead child from the hospital. But in my current state all I could really think was, *This poor woman . . .* and *Holy fuck, I'm going to die!*

Abruptly she wiped the tears from her face and flipped to the back of the book. She added the two photos she'd taken of me to the book. She stood and dropped the photo album back on the table and pushed all the furniture to the edge of the room before disappearing down the hallway.

There were the sounds of items being moved around, followed by a crinkling noise. When she returned she was carrying a blue tarp. She didn't look at me as she unfolded the tarp and laid it in the middle of the room. She left the room again, this time disappearing into the kitchen. She returned with a small, brown glass bottle. She dipped an eyedropper into its contents before squeezing and releasing the rubber bulb top to fill it.

My heart kicked into overdrive. I had to do something. I tried with everything I had to move or say something but all I managed were some unintelligible grunts she ignored. And as panicked as I was, my breathing felt as though it was slowing down.

Tonya grabbed my forehead and shoved it back roughly before

forcing the glass dropper between my lips and squirting a salty tasting liquid into my mouth. With no control over my tongue the liquid slid down my throat and I knew I only had minutes to live. My mind raced as the knowledge of impending death settled in. Sadly, I couldn't think of a single person who'd miss me when I was gone and I wondered how long it would be before someone noticed. Rent wasn't due for another two weeks. And I was certain the landlord would assume I just flaked out and dodged the rent by disappearing. The only solace I could settle on was that they would eventually find her if they looked at my computer, cell phone history, or debit card transactions. Tonya was definitely unhinged but luckily she didn't appear to be a mastermind of deception or she would've gotten rid of my cellphone before we made it here or insisted she pay with cash or not take a cab. It's a funny thing . . . accepting death as your only option. Because whether or not the police discovered what Tonya did, the damage was already done.

Tonya grabbed my ankles and began to drag me off the sofa and onto the floor. My thinking began to grow fuzzier, my hearing sounded as if I'd slipped into a pool of water, and darkness was eating at the edges of my vision. And all I could think was, *I should've swiped left.*

GATES OF HELL

GATES of HELL

"ALSO KNOWN AS THE 'Portal to Hell' or the 'Blood Bowl'. It was given the latter name when a skateboarder died there back in the 1980s while trying to perform a trick inside the tunnel," Brian said. He took a sip of his coffee and used the thumb of the hand holding his cell phone to scroll down the page. He picked up a donut hole without taking his eyes off what he was reading and popped the sugar-covered dough in his mouth, chewed it a few times, and spoke around it. "It used to be a popular spot for skateboarders but technically you're not supposed to go there. We could get in trouble for trespassing if anyone sees us."

"Uh-huh," Laura said.

Laura propped her chin in the palm of her hand before setting her elbow on the greasy and hastily wiped down table. She watched the teenagers bustling behind the counter to help the customers at the drive-thru with their coffee, latte, and donut orders. Each of the workers appeared so young and inexperienced. Not just inexperienced at their jobs but in life as a whole. High school kids. And Laura noted they weren't much younger than herself.

"Are you listening?" Brian said with an air of agitation.

"Huh?" Laura sat up straight and turned her attention to Brian. He looked peeved. "Sorry," she said and used her usual excuse. "I'm a little tired from the drive." She lifted her coffee and took a sip to punctuate her excuse, burning the tip of her tongue in the process. Going to college and working part-time kept her on the brink of total exhaustion during the school year. Luckily, she was off for summer break at the moment, but that didn't stop her from using her usual excuse. Wasn't everyone tired?

Brian sighed. "When we leave, we'll have to make sure no one sees us sneak over the fence. Someone might call the cops on us."

Laura looked at the workers again. "I don't really think anyone working here gives a shit. They're probably more interested in what friends they're going to hang out with when they get a day off."

Brian turned his attention to the workers. "Yeah. But we'll have to make sure no one driving by or anyone in the drive-thru sees us. I don't want to get slapped with trespassing and have to deal with the cops." He popped another donut hole in his mouth before turning his attention back to his phone. "The legend says there's more than one gates to Hell. Some say there are seven and if you pass through all of them you will go straight to Hell. Other legends state that to pass through one will take you to the underworld. But one thing is for sure. There is a ritual or key to open the gates and no one knows what it is. Some believe you need to sacrifice a virgin or you need virgin blood." His eyes flicked up to her briefly before reading on.

Laura chose to ignore him. It wasn't something she wanted to discuss in public. She knew how odd it was in this day and age to still be a virgin at twenty years old but she didn't think she was ready. The thought of losing her virginity came with so much anxiety. How bad would it hurt? Would she bleed? Would whoever took her virginity be worthy of it and would they stick around? She didn't have any religious qualms that stopped her from having sex. It made her feel like she had control over one sacred thing in her life and it made her feel empowered and she was afraid it would diminish her in some capacity or another if she let it go too quick. She'd told him when they first started dating and thankfully Brian hadn't pressured her at all. She wasn't shy about telling the guys she dated but most of them saw it as a challenge and got angry and dumped her after some undetermined amount of time the man thought was ample enough for her to put out. She imagined the reason Brian hadn't left her yet was because he'd lost his virginity when he was sixteen to his high school sweetheart who'd dumped him after graduation so she could "explore her options" in college. Laura knew she'd be naive to think Brian wasn't well-practiced in the art of masturbation. If that's what kept him from hounding her for sex then so be it. She could only hope he didn't eventually decide to move on to someone with less hang-ups like every other guy.

Laura feigned interest in what Brian was reading but in actuality she could care less. She'd agreed to the five-hour ride so she could wallow in some record stores after he was done filming some horse-shit urban legend story he'd found online. Brian wanted her to come along and be the cameraperson and record his exploration of the Gates of Hell for his YouTube channel, the main focus of which was on urban legends. Horror or fantasy or whatever it was he was into wasn't exactly Laura's thing, but it *was* Brian's thing, and she tried her best not to act like she was miserable whenever he rattled on about some place or another he wanted to visit. She encouraged him to do the things he loved and went along for the ride because she knew Brian made concessions for her too. The urban legends all seemed pretty boring to her. She'd rather be at home, lying on the sofa, listening to records and reading a book, but she wanted to spend as much time with him as possible before college returned in the fall. It was hard to tell if it was love she was feeling since they'd only been dating for four months, but she thought she should at least put some effort into the relationship even if she wasn't into everything he was into.

"Look at these photos," he said.

He turned his phone's screen toward her so she could see an image of a heavily graffitied tunnel opening. Someone had spray painted the mouth of the tunnel to look like a yellow, triangle-headed monster with three eyes and four sharp, off-center teeth. The entire face of the tunnel's entrance, and what could be seen of the tunnel before darkness enveloped it, was covered in layers upon layers of graffiti. One particular piece, a red smiley face with an inverted cross on its forehead, made her feel uneasy for some inexplicable reason. Brian swiped his finger on the screen to show her a few other photos of the chaotic artwork.

"Creepy," Laura said.

Brian smiled to himself as he looked at a few other photos. He trained his eyes on the last donut hole and then at her. Laura knew he wanted it but was trying to offer it to her since it was the last one.

"You can have it," she said. "I'm not really hungry."

He pocketed his phone and ate the last hole. He grabbed a napkin from the dispenser on their table and wiped his mouth. He nodded at her coffee. "You've barely touched that."

"I'm taking it with me." She felt the sides of the paper cup to find out if it had cooled down since her last sip. It felt less likely to burn her tongue so she took another sip.

He nodded. "Are you ready then? Need the restroom before we go?"

"Yeah, let me stop in the ladies' room first."

"Sure," he said. He stood, pulled on his backpack, and grabbed her coffee. "I'll meet you outside."

Once she was done in the restroom, she found Brian standing beside their car in the parking lot. He handed her the coffee when she approached. The temperature of the paper cup had cooled considerably and was easier to handle.

"Ready?" he asked.

She nodded before taking a drink of her coffee.

Brian scanned the parking lot and drive-thru. "Let's go."

He started toward the wooden privacy fence behind the coffee shop and slipped behind a brick structure that housed the dumpster once he reached it. Laura followed him closely, and once they were behind the brick structure and hidden from view, she tossed her coffee cup over the wall for the dumpster. A slap and splash could be heard and she knew she'd missed her target.

Brian said, "What'd you do that for?"

He appeared peeved and she assumed it was because *he'd* paid for the overpriced swill. She wasn't going to choke it down only because he'd paid for it. Her mom used to bitch at her for not eating everything on her plate, regardless if she hated it, and Laura could never understand being hounded about not finishing something.

"Sorry, that stuff tasted awful. Like they burned the beans or something. Besides, I can't climb over the fence and hold the cup at the same time."

"I could've climbed over and you could've handed it to me."

"Sorry," she repeated.

He ran his hand through his hair, mumbled something about her being a coffee snob, and shook his head before sighing. His reaction made her uncomfortable and she felt heat rising in her face.

She could tell he was irritated, which was unusual for him. Why was he so upset over a stupid coffee? She'd watched him throw tons of perfectly fine leftovers in the garbage instead of asking for a doggie bag when they went out. She didn't think he was much of a frugal person up to that point, but if he wanted to throw a fit about it, she'd give him the damn money he spent on it.

And then it happened. She knew it the moment it happened in every relationship. It was jarring and quick, but overall, it always made her feel disappointed. This wasn't going to last. The moment a guy made her feel bad about something she'd said or done, or over something she liked, she knew the relationship was doomed. It was like a definitive end to the honeymoon stage. The last day of a vacation when you stepped on the plane to go home. The "this was nice but now it's over" slap in the face. It always stung a little each time. But it also got easier each time to automatically shut down emotionally when it happened. No sense in getting attached because it wouldn't last forever. She started every relationship with a blank slate, not allowing what any other guy had done or said to affect the next. But sadly, she was starting to think they were all the same. She didn't know if that said something about her or about them. Was it her fault she somehow managed to end up with the same type of guy each time or were men really all the same?

Without another word, he grabbed the top of the fence, found a toe hold between the slats, and boosted himself over. She followed exactly what he'd done and he helped her over. The other side of the fence was populated with a dense swath of honeysuckle. Laura remembered reading somewhere that honeysuckle was an invasive species because it grew so dense and quick their roots strangled out other trees native to the area. She scanned the tree tops and noticed the telltale signs that the larger trees were dying. Giants strangled by dwarves.

Brian began to push his way through the brush and Laura followed him. The branches scraped her arms, hands, and legs and she wished she'd worn pants instead of shorts. She briefly worried about getting poison ivy until Brian let go of a particularly springy branch and it smacked her in the face. She yelped in pain but he didn't seem to notice or care and proceeded to bumble through the overgrowth.

Yeah, she thought, *this isn't gonna work if this is how he's gonna act over a cup of coffee.*

The flush of embarrassment/disappointment she'd felt earlier intensified. Her skin felt prickly and damp and her shirt clung to her back. Sure, it was summer, but today wasn't particularly hot. And they were in the shade. A bead of sweat ran down the side of her face and she noticed her heart was racing and her mouth was very dry. *The coffee must've been jacked up on caffeine*, she thought.

Finally, they broke through the trees and into a concrete clearing. Two large metal structures, resembling heavy-duty fences constructed from I-beams she hadn't seen in the photos, sat on either side of the tunnel's opening. The I-beams were also covered in layers of graffiti. With the tunnel wall as one side, the two metal structures were angled toward each other to create a triangle and the tip pointed directly at them. There was a gap where the two fences should've met and there was enough room for someone to squeeze through.

"What is that?" Laura said.

"It's to catch trash and branches when it rains," Brian said. "If we walk through the tunnel there's a stream on the other side. All the garbage would clog the tunnel or end up in the stream."

Only then did she take note of all the fast-food wrappers, empty beer cans, cigarette packs, bicycle parts, and tree branches piled against the bottoms of the I-beams. She also spotted what she thought was a smashed disposable hospital urinal and her face screwed up in revulsion. She hoped there weren't any syringes lying around, waiting to be accidentally stepped on.

The two approached the I-beam structure. Brian pulled his backpack off before slipping through the gap in the structure. Laura followed him and stared at the graffiti while Brian retrieved the camera stand from his backpack. The yellow triangle monster painted over the entrance from the photo was gone. It had been replaced with a devil's head. The tunnel was its open and inviting mouth.

Laura felt like she was roasting and tried to fan herself with her hand but the gesture was pointless. She resorted to pulling the collar of her t-shirt up over her face and blotting the sweat with the inside of her shirt. She felt like she could run a marathon. But there was something else happening she didn't want to admit. Laura was growing aroused and it was starting to make her a bit agitated.

Brian attached his cell phone to the tripod, keeping the legs folded in so it took on the appearance of an oversized staff, and fiddled with a few buttons on the cell. A light on the phone turned on and blinded

Laura as he turned it toward her.

"Okay," he said. "I think we're ready to go. All you have to do is hit the start button and it'll start streaming live to my channel. Here." He extended the tripod to her.

"I don't feel too good." She wiped her brow with the back of her hand. "I think the coffee was too strong. Can we do this another time?" She fidgeted and was overly aware of how wet her sex had become. She was afraid that before too long a visible spot would appear in the seat of her shorts.

"No." He still held the camera out to her and gave it a shake. "I came all this way for this. I've been teasing this to my subscribers for months. It'll only take a few minutes, I promise. Then we can do whatever you want."

She wanted to complain or walk away but she knew it would be easier and quicker to film him for his show and have him take her home afterward. She was also mulling over if she should break it off with him when she got home. It was becoming more apparent that Brian was pretty self-involved and she knew it wasn't going to work out. It was better to end it sooner than later. It was also better for her emotionally if she broke it off with him before he dumped her.

She hesitantly took the camera stand. For one brief and crazed moment she contemplated rubbing herself against one of the aluminum legs. Never in her life had she felt so horny and it was maddening. She wondered if her thoughts about Brian were harsh only because she was aroused and frustrated. Maybe she should wait a few days before breaking up with him. Maybe once she was in a normal state of mind everything would look different.

Laura opened the tripod's legs, adjusted the height, and made sure Brian was in the frame. She looked at him for confirmation that he was ready and he nodded. She touched the red square on the cell phone's screen and it began to blink and a time appeared as the top of the screen and began counting. She gave Brian a thumbs-up to convey the camera was rolling and everything looked okay.

"Hey, folks! Welcome back to Exploring Urban Legends with Brian. As promised, I'm streaming live from the Gates of Hell." He waved at the entrance of the tunnel and started walking backward toward it, still facing the camera as he spoke. "So, as I'd mentioned in the previous video, if you haven't seen that video just click on my channel—" he pointed down with both index fingers to the general area where the viewer would find the information he was talking about "—and don't forget to like and subscribe while you're there, but in my previous video I talked about the Gates of Hell." He stopped at the tunnel's entrance. "There are several urban legends about the many different Gates of Hell." He steepled his fingers as he talked. "I'm hoping to visit all of them some day. But for now, we're going to explore the one closest to where I live. This one is located in Trainsville, behind Billy's Coffee and Donuts in the downtown area. If you check out Trip Advisor you can see several photos of the constantly transforming graffiti." He looked over his shoulder at the tunnel's entrance before addressing the camera. "The devil's head seems fitting. Anyway, the legend states that this is an entrance to Hell but there is a specific ritual to open it and no one knows for sure what that ritual is. Others say that in order to open it you would have to either open all the other gates throughout the world one at a time or synchronize a group of people to perform the ritual at each location at the exact same time. Either way, let's check this one out." He turned to enter the tunnel and waved at Laura to follow him with the camera.

It was becoming increasingly difficult for Laura to concentrate on what she was supposed to be doing. Her level of arousal was more than anything she'd ever experienced. She lifted the camera by the tripod stand, trying to keep it level and focused on Brian, and carefully followed him inside the mouth of the devil. The cool interior of the tunnel felt good against her flushed and sweaty skin. She focused on Brian's image on the phone screen and carefully set the stand down, making sure the shot was as straight as possible. He pointed to some of the graffiti and talked for a minute or two but Laura couldn't focus on much more than the turmoil her body was going through and wasn't able to concentrate on what he was saying.

Brian started to make his way farther down the tunnel. She grabbed the tripod and followed him. It was beginning to grow more difficult to see. The phone's light wasn't the greatest. Brian pulled off his backpack and retrieved a small battery-powered lantern and switched it on, revealing a bend farther down the tunnel. Someone had painted a green arrow pointing toward the righthand bend and the words "HELL HERE" above the arrow.

Laura started to feel disoriented and tried to collect herself. It dawned on her that she needed to show the people watching all the artwork on the walls. Brian continued his story about the history of the urban legend as they approached the turn in the tunnel. She swept the camera along the walls slowly, allowing the viewer to see all of the designs. Mostly the artwork consisted of people's names, curse words, penises, pentagrams, and badly rendered and outdated cartoons.

Once they rounded the bend in the tunnel, the daylight from the opening was cut off. The absence of daylight made the tunnel feel more oppressing to Laura. Something about the darkness felt like a wet velvet tongue against every inch of her body. Her skin felt like it was crawling and swollen, as if she could bust out of it at any moment. Brian had stopped walking and she set the tripod down. It took her a few more seconds to realize he'd also stopped talking and was looking at her expectantly. She double-checked the phone's screen and it displayed Brian standing beside a spray-painted silhouette of a man with horns.

Brian said, "Come here." He waved for Laura to join him.

She shook her head and didn't say anything. She wanted to tell him she didn't want to be on his show but she also didn't want to interrupt the recording. Laura wasn't sure how she looked but she knew how she felt and she wasn't sure if it would show up on the recording. Also, the thought of getting close to Brian suddenly frightened her. She'd never been so horny in her entire life and, with each second that passed, she was becoming more agreeable with the idea to scratch that itch. It wasn't that she was afraid of Brian. She was afraid of herself. She wasn't quite sure what she would do if he touched her. *Hell*, she thought, *even just smelling him might break something inside of me*. And the caffeine wasn't helping anything. If it was the caffeine. It sure didn't feel like any caffeine buzz she'd ever experienced. She was sweating bullets and her heart was racing and her pussy was wanting more than it ever had.

"Please," he said.

Laura lifted the collar of her shirt and blotted her face before reluctantly joining Brian. She hoped she didn't look like a crazed sweaty monster on camera. The closer Laura got to Brian, the more she felt like her body was vibrating. She stopped a couple of feet from him and hoped she wasn't in the frame.

He grabbed her hand and pulled her against his body. He turned to the camera. "This is my girlfriend, Laura. Say hello to everyone."

Laura lifted her hand and gave a half-hearted wave. "Hello."

He placed his lips near her earlobe and whispered, "Don't be shy."

His breath on her damp skin sent a new surge of desire and heat raging through her body. She didn't refuse him when he kissed her lightly on the neck. His touch unlocked something within her. She was only vaguely aware they were being watched but nothing seemed to matter anymore. She pulled his mouth to hers. His tongue was cool against hers as the kissing quickly became aggressive and desperate. The camera didn't bother her and seemed to be of little importance as she unfastened Brian's pants. He moaned softly into her mouth as they kissed and the approving sound he made increased the frenzy within her. She didn't know what was coming over her and it was futile to try and stop it.

His hands were up her shirt, unfastening her bra. She was pulling off his shirt. Clothes littered the tunnel floor as they finished undressing one another. Laura caught Brian glancing at the camera and a flitting thought came to her: *His show is going to get banned.*

Laura pulled her mouth from his. She was breathing heavily and it felt like she couldn't get enough air. "Please, I can't stop. I'm ready."

She pressed her back against the tunnel, knowing she was up against the silhouette of the horned man, and pulled Brian to her before lifting one leg and wrapping it around his waist. He placed his hands on the back of her thighs to support her as she wrapped the other leg around his waist. He stopped short of entering her.

"Please," she begged him. "I have to."

Without a word, he entered her slowly. The shock of the unfamiliar sensation, a cramp of pain, and a slight sting in her sex caused her whole body to shutter. This was it. She was no longer a virgin. Laura was equally overwhelmed and underwhelmed. She'd known what to expect from the stories her girlfriends had told her but, for some odd reason, she thought there would be more. She thought there would be a moment of enlightenment or a spark or something that would mark the catastrophic end of her purity. There was nothing but raw lust and skin on skin and the smell of her sex with a hint of copper. *Isn't there more than this?* she thought.

Brian began to thrust slowly. "You okay?" he whispered as though he didn't want to be detected by the microphone.

Her cunt pulsed with desire. "I can't stop." She pressed her mons pubis against him and the pressure on her clit exasperated the fire within her. The cool concrete against her back felt good as she ground against him.

He kissed her neck and said, "Don't worry."

"Wha . . ." She was so enveloped in the moment it was making it hard for her to concentrate. She felt dizzy and disoriented. *Don't worry?* "Don't worry," she managed to say.

"Here," he said, grabbing her hand and moving it toward her sex. "I want you to play with yourself. You know how to do you."

Laura did what he asked of her and knew the orgasm was just

under the surface. Something was expanding in her. Something red hot and acidic was just below her skin. Her pussy was swollen and slick and all the sensations were too much to take. Pleasure and pain. And before she could realize what was happening, she was coming. The orgasm ripped through her, causing her whole body to convulse with each pulse of pleasure. She yelped at the unexpected sensation and suddenly felt the euphoria she'd heard so much about. Brian made an agreeable sound and his thrusting quickened. Each wave of pleasure Laura experienced was more intense than the previous and, suddenly, with each wave came a searing pain that started in her diaphragm.

"Something is happening," Laura said.

"Almost," Brian grunted as he fucked her.

The burning sensation began to spread through her body. "Something's not right," she said. The pain was becoming more intense and her body felt like it was on fire. Her skin was slick with sweat and Brian was having a hard time keeping a hold on her thighs as his exertions were causing him to sweat too.

"Almost there."

"Brian, something's happen—"

He cried out as he came inside her, startling her. It was the last sound she'd ever hear from him again.

Laura screamed as her cunt split open, ripping up to her ribcage. Rows upon rows of teeth sprouted along the edges of her new sex and clamped down on Brian as she pulled his body tight to hers. The look of shock on his face was comical and she laughed with a voice that wasn't hers. Brian's blood splattered all over Laura and the tunnel walls.

Laura's skin was suddenly too small to contain her anymore. Her skin cracked as whatever lay beneath began to swell. She roared as new, longer, sharper fingers exploded from the ends of her fingertips. The pain consumed her and her mind went primal.

Attack what is causing the pain. Kill it. Stop it.

Brian's face was a pale mask of terror and he opened his mouth but nothing came out. He took a step back from her and his intestines spilled from the gaping wound her new cunt had created. She felt Brian's severed penis fall from her vagina. She lunged at him and wrapped her hands around his neck and squeezed. He clawed at her hands weakly but it was pointless. He fell to the ground in shock. Laura went down with him and straddled him as she tried to choke the last bit of life out of him. He'd done this to her. He'd destroyed her body and now she was going to end him.

A massive headache ripped through both of her temples and a sickening crunch vibrated through her skull. She briefly wondered if the top of her head had exploded.

A tremendous rush of air howled through the tunnel, knocking the tripod over. The wind ripped the split and ruined skin from Laura's body, exposing something that had never stepped foot on earth.

The spray-painted silhouette on the tunnel wall began to reshape itself, swirling, stretching, opening. Inside the opening was darker than the bottom of the ocean. The screams of millions echoed and belched from within, fighting their way through the wind pouring into the abyss. The tripod was sucked into the hole. The lantern was caught in the crook of Brian's neck, illuminating both of their faces.

The wind pushed the entangled duo toward the gaping hole. The concrete ripped at the skin on Brian's back, smearing more blood on the tunnel floor. He lifted his hand weakly and tried to swipe at Laura's face but there wasn't much fight left in him. Laura could see the life fading from his eyes.

The force of the wind knocked crumbling concrete within the tunnel loose. The flying debris pummeled Laura and Brian as it tried to make its way past them and into the opening.

Laura let go of Brian's neck and dug her hands into his ruined stomach. She savagely divested him from any remaining organs. He had caused her metamorphosis and she knew nothing would ever be the same. In one clean yank she ripped his heart from his body. She noted a missing element in his eyes as she showed him how repugnant it was. Brian was already dead.

A final gust of wind flushed through the tunnel, lifting the couple and the lantern, and flinging them into the bottomless void. The light flickered and went out as Laura plunged into the darkness. She briefly wondered if the gates would stay open forever as the million screams became her new home.

ENDLESS FLESH

△▽△▽△▽ **WAS THE SECOND TO** last performer to take the stage at Cyc0 Cynics. I'd been a fan of theirs for years and it was hard not to gush when I finally saw them backstage. A short, thin wraith in a hoodie pulled so low I could only see their unsmiling lips and their long, limp, black hair cascading down their chest. The lips were full yet thin. Hair lustrous but unkempt. Sex was indeterminate but it didn't matter. I mean . . . it was △▽△▽△▽ and I was finally going to perform on Cyc0 Cynics' stage for the first time. I'd turned them down at least ten times, a formality of contrarianism for any reclusive musician. It all felt so surreal. I'd never performed live for a number of reasons: nervousness, the whole mysterious anonymity of each performer was unique and I had no idea if what I'd chosen was hack or not, and my performances were . . . unpredictable and best kept in the privacy of my basement where I had complete control.

I stood in the doorway on the righthand side of the stage. Three short steps and I could be on stage with △▽△▽△▽ as they finished their set by performing "Infinit3 S4dn3ZZ." It was the last song on the first side of their debut LP album, *Broken † Soul*. The slow build of the opening bass notes made the crowd restless and I felt full of anticipation for the screaming cacophony that took over midway through the composition. I'd always wondered how they'd managed to produce such a harsh and overpowering sound until I stumbled across a random music blog online.

△▽△▽△▽'s table was full. A laptop sat on a stand and a purple, ethereal glow from the screen lit the bottom half of their face, the only light in the entire place. I could barely make out the glint of light reflecting off the ten-gallon aquarium positioned beside the laptop as △▽△▽△▽ lifted a square box, illuminated with a dim red light, into the air. The crowd went crazy as △▽△▽△▽ held up the box containing the microphone.

Someone shouted, "Do it! Come on!"

△▽△▽△▽ hit a couple of buttons on their laptop—the reverb and whatever additional side effects that created the noise that came next—and slammed the boxed microphone down into the aquarium I knew was filled with broken glass. A shrill and deafening sound made the speakers shudder and pop loud enough to make me wonder if anyone had ever blown them. Half the crowd put their fingers in their ears. The other half had been smart enough to wear earplugs. Any fan of △▽△▽△▽ would've known to wear earplugs.

Overtop the din of amplified glass breaking, a low, slow voice chanted, "My broken soul. My broken soul. My broken soul." The speed of the vocals was slowed to the point of sexlessness. And who knew if it was actually △▽△▽△▽ or dialog from some obscure movie or a sound clip they'd found online. All I knew was "Infinit3 S4dn3ZZ" was my favorite song of theirs.

The music filled me with an energy and I had to refrain from moving to the music. Nothing, I mean nothing, was lamer in our small world than another musician dancing, or even nodding, to the beat of another band's music. Dancing, in general, was not considered cool unless you were in the crowd and showing any sign of admiration was not part of the scene. Anonymity and no emotions. You had to act as though everyone else sucked.

I stayed rooted where I stood as △▽△▽△▽ finished their set. Once they were done playing, they pulled a large, wheeled suitcase out from under the table and quickly disassembled their setup, stuffing everything into the suitcase with no regard to the cost of the equipment. Two Cyc0 Cynics employees appeared on stage with headlamps on. They each grabbed one end of the now empty table and walked it behind the black backdrop before retrieving another table, which held all of my equipment. △▽△▽△▽ exited the stage while the tables were being swapped, pulling their suitcase hurriedly, and letting it bounce down the three steps leading to the backstage door. I pulled on my hood to make sure there was no way △▽△▽△▽ could see my face as they passed me.

After a few seconds, I stepped back into the green room. △▽△▽△▽ was already halfway down the hall that led to the alley out back. No one else was in the room. I was the last one to perform. *How the fuck did I go from a nobody to a headliner without ever playing live?* I thought. I looked at all the flyers tacked to the walls with the lists of performers that had played tonight and so many other nights before.

□■∞○○∞■□

\/0I▲

▼▲GIN▲∞▼IRÇINS

ZΛ†ΛN HOVS3

FL3SH CvLT

‡BTCHKRFT‡

GЯ4V3¥4ЯD S¥N†H

ME△T TR△SH

GHXST FVCKER

△▽△▽△▽

The door flew open before I could find my name.

One of the two club workers stood in the doorway with his head-lamp still switched on. "You're up."

I took a deep breath and tried not to think about the crowd. I had to focus and not be nervous as I climbed the three stairs to the stage. I lifted the hem of my black cloak to keep from tripping on it and worried my outfit was too goofy. I had to be calm. I'd never get all the equipment set up and be able to play if my hands were shaking.

The lights from the workers' head lamps swept over my equipment. The crowd ignored me and talked amongst themselves, their faces empty and haunting under the illumination of their cell phones. The toilets seemed to constantly flush. Being part of the crowd at Cyc0 Cynics was one thing. It didn't matter if the place was pitch-black if you were an attendee. But setting up as a musician, as I was discovering, was a pain in the ass.

I directed one of the workers to plug in the projector and position it so it faced the black backdrop, which, without playing the DVD, lit up the stage with a bright white light where the image should play. I hurriedly hooked up my equipment and lights with my head down, hiding my face. The two workers left me to finish the job. I'd practiced setting up several times at home, in low lighting, until I could do it in under five minutes. Once the table was set, I hurried to the projector, popped in the DVD, and hit play. The club darkened considerably as purple swirls replaced the blank white square on the backdrop. The purple roamed over the fabric and my name was displayed in the center in white: ẄI†CH • C▼N†

Either my name or the display or the anticipation riled up a few girls who took the opportunity to hoot and woo. It was the end of the night. They were most likely high or drunk.

I took my position behind the table, opened my laptop and deftly opened everything I would need. I took a deep breath and began to play "P4ndor4's Box." A low droning emanated from the speakers and I slowly added the prerecorded and mixed synth. I saw the songs as layers and started to build the sound, increasing its intensity, allowing it to go on for longer than it needed to, and at the moment I unleashed the throbbing techno beat I hit the black lights on the table. The low light from the projector was enough that I could make out the faces of the people in the front couple of rows.

The DayGlo green face paint on my cheeks was activated by the blacklight and at first it screwed with my vision until my eyes adjusted. I pulled my hood back so the crowd could see the green glowing skull I'd painted on my face. The crowd began to pulse and dance to the music. I added the distorted tinkling of a music box to the mix.

My fingers began to tingle and I knew then the night wouldn't end well. I was suddenly filled with regret but there was no turning back now. The spell of the music had taken over. I hesitated for a second before laying into the small synthesizer to the right of the laptop. What came from the instrument was beyond my control. The energy from the crowd was building as they swayed and danced in the darkness. The music morphed into something dark, sinister, and methodical. The song went on and on and on. Time meant nothing. Finally, the frenzy of the crowd began to slow. People in the front stopped dancing and they all turned their attention to the backdrop beyond me. They stared openmouthed and unmoving and I knew the stage was set.

I peeked over my shoulder at the backdrop. The swirls of purple had grown brighter and were snaking from the backdrop and slithering across the stage. One of the tentacles made its way toward me. I knew better than to fight it and turned back to the keys. It pushed its way under my cloak and encircled me, climbing higher, and splitting into two parts at the base of my neck before making its way down both of my arms.

I leaned toward the microphone positioned in front of the synth and spoke softly. "Are you ready to enter the void? She's been waiting for you. She wants to be filled but is destined to be gaping." I hit a button on the synthesizer to start the two infrasonic sound combinations I'd accidently discovered the night I'd written the song. I could feel it and knew everyone else in the room could feel it too. It made all of my bones vibrate and the pressure it created made it difficult to breathe and my ears felt clogged.

A few of the people in the front row flinched and snapped out of their trance once the streams of purple touched them. They started to back away from the stage. Panic set in. Someone in the crowd screamed. This is what they asked for. They wanted me to perform? They were about to see the performance of a lifetime. Something that would be talked about for years to come. A song that some had heard a hundred times but had never seen performed live. And there was a reason for that.

"Don't be scared," I said into the microphone. "You'll be happy once it's over. Give in to her and let her take you."

The air in the room was suddenly sucked toward the backdrop. I checked over my shoulder again as the triangle in the name began to open. The cords from my equipment came unplugged but the music still played, increasing in volume and taking over. The cords waved wildly in the air, shooting sparks from their ends, before darting toward the crowd, wrapping around some of the attendees, lifting them into the air, and tossing them toward the growing opening in the backdrop. The purple streams followed the cords' lead. People were tossed, screaming, into the expanding portal.

The tentacles manipulated me and the music before they lifted me from the ground. I didn't fight it as I was thrown into the portal along with everyone else in the room. I went limp and felt the normal sting, similar to a sunburn, when I entered.

We became a tangled mass of bodies. People screamed and panicked, swimming through the jelly I'd become accustomed to. I'd found it soothing the first time but apparently the crowd did not.

I shouted, "Don't panic! When it's over you'll feel invigorated!"

No one listened. They were lost in their terror. Hands, limbs, torsos, and faces flashed before mine. All of them grasping for something to hold on to, clawing at the void. Faces filled with horror. I felt a smile creeping across my lips. The chaos felt normal and delightful. No one would forget this.

A young girl's face appeared before me. The horror in her

expression made her beautiful and I wanted to kiss her.

"Don't fight her," I said. "It'll be over soon."

And then she was gone. Replaced by an arm, a foot, a torso. Replaced by endless flesh.

The group rocked back and forth. Back and forth. She was thrusting us within her. She was using us to be satiated. Back and forth. Back and forth. Eventually the portal squeezed the mass of people and quivered, pulsed, and relaxed before tensing again and again, each time the constriction becoming fainter. I relaxed as we were all shoved toward the entrance. The group stopped short of the portal opening.

"Relax!" I shouted over the commotion. "You can't exit if you're fighting her!"

I wasn't sure if I'd be able to leave if the whole group didn't act in tandem. I went limp and was pushed through the group as they all continued to squirm and resist. I was dumped unceremoniously onto the stage outside of the portal. Purple goo saturated my cloak and covered my body. I collapsed in a fit of joyous laughter as the euphoria washed over me. The feeling was greater than an orgasm. A feeling of such great pleasure it was painful. The pain I associated with knowing the sensation would come to an end soon. It never lasted long. The music still played but the venue was empty, except for myself.

When I regained myself, I turned my attention to the portal. The swimming mass of people were at the edge but none of them could get through. They struggled in the slime as the edges of the doorway began to shrink.

"Shit," I muttered.

A burly man with black hair was able to grab the edge of the portal. "What's happening?" he shouted over the music. He strained to reach out of the portal, offering me his hand as if I could help, but he wasn't strong enough. "Help me!"

"You have to relax! She won't let go until you do! I'm not sure what will happen if the door closes!"

He let go of the portal's edge and was sucked back into the crowd. The purple fog on the stage began to retract back into the doorway. More people began to scream as they realized the portal was closing. I yelled for them to go limp but none of them listened. The people toward the front stretched out their hands for help. I'd never been closed inside and didn't know if everyone would still be there when I opened it again. I assumed everyone would've enjoyed the ride the way I did the first time I'd accidentally opened it. A music experience like no other. I figured they'd be overcome with the wonder of it all and would've been spat out with no problems. But they were fighting it. I desperately yelled instructions to them even as the portal finally closed.

The music stopped on its own and the room became quiet except for my own heavy breathing. The light from the projector, my laptop, and the blacklights on the table were the only light again.

A toilet flushed in the distance. I turned my attention toward the bathrooms. A few moments passed before the men's room door opened. A silhouette appeared in the lighted doorway, then disappeared as a person stepped out of the bathroom, the door closing behind them. There was a faint echo of footfalls as he crossed the floor. *How long was this person in the bathroom?* I thought. Out of the darkness a man appeared. His expression was confused as he approached the stage. He stared at me for a moment, taking in my disheveled state.

"Where did everyone go?"

"Um, uh . . . Inside the witch cunt."

We stared at one another awkwardly. His eyes were glassy and bloodshot.

He drew out his response. "O . . . K . . . ?" He began to step backward, away from me, disappearing back into the darkness of the venue.

I said, "Don't forget to tell your friends."

Other Grindhouse Press Titles

www.ingramcontent.com/pod-product-compliance
Lightning Source LLC
Chambersburg PA
CBHW011451170626
46814CB00012B/3086